SAVANNAH MED

VIGILANTES FOR JUSTICE
BOOK FIVE

ALAN CHAPUT

PREVIOUSLY IN THE VIGILANTES FOR JUSTICE SERIES

Savannah Sleuth (Book One): Patricia's darling mother, a prominent philanthropist, drops dead, and the police are baffled by her untimely death. Patricia recruits her three friends to help her investigate what she believes is murder. Savannah Sleuth is a page-turning journey from Savannah's Southern wealth and grace into the hidden corners of Savannah and across two continents in a deadly pursuit of justice.

Savannah Secrets (Book Two): When Patricia Falcon's husband Trey is kidnapped, she is plunged into a complex race that crosses continents and decades and will push her to her emotional and mental limits. Patricia's investigative talents are further challenged because her husband's ransom isn't money. Desperate to ensure the safe return of Trey, Patricia reaches out to a Catholic bishop, a local witch doctor, and two secret organizations hoping to piece together the clues she needs to find and deliver what the kidnappers want before it's too late.

Savannah Justice (Book Three): At the urging of a close friend, amateur sleuth Patricia Falcon investigates a massive, fast growing private investment plan and discovers serious irregularities that could shake the financial foundations of many of her friends and most of Savannah's major institutions. When things take a stunning turn, Patricia finds herself in the midst of something much more serious, and she may well be the prime suspect.

Savannah Dragon (Book Four): While investigating the murder of her longtime hairdresser, amateur sleuth Patricia Falcon stumbles into a crisis of epic proportions. Her city has been infiltrated and the roots go years deep. It feels like every case she's worked has been leading to this one. Because she's the only one who sees the connection and the danger. Can Patricia and her team quickly gather enough evidence to convince the FBI to take decisive action before all of Savannah falls to its knees and, perhaps, takes the rest of the nation with it?

CHAPTER 1

Patricia Falcon guided her latest rescue—a frail woman with hollow eyes and a faded bruise shadowing her cheekbone—into the cramped lobby of the shelter. The smell of stale coffee and the faint chemical tang of cleaning products hung in the air, mingling with the low hum of voices and the occasional scrape of chairs against the worn linoleum floor. A volunteer at the front desk glanced up with a welcoming smile.

The woman hesitated, her thin fingers trembling as they gripped the straps of her tattered bag. Patricia gently placed a hand on her shoulder, steadying her. "It's okay," Patricia murmured softly. "You're not alone anymore."

The woman nodded but didn't meet Patricia's eyes. Together, they approached the desk, where a kind-looking volunteer introduced herself and slid a clipboard across the counter.

"Just a few things to fill out, sweetheart," the volunteer said, her voice warm but professional. "Take your time."

Patricia stayed by her side as the woman clumsily worked through the paperwork, her pen faltering. Her breaths were shallow, her shoulders curled inward as if trying to make herself invisible. Patricia watched the way the woman's hair, limp and unevenly cut, fell over her face like a curtain.

"Need any help with that?" Patricia asked gently, leaning closer.

The woman shook her head without looking up. "No. I—I can do it." Her voice was barely above a whisper.

The minutes stretched out until, finally, the woman handed the clipboard back with shaky hands. The volunteer gave her a reassuring smile. "Welcome, honey. We're going to take good care of you."

The woman turned to Patricia then, her bloodshot eyes glistening with unshed tears. She hesitated for a moment, as if unsure whether she was allowed to show gratitude, then stepped forward and wrapped her arms around Patricia in a tentative, almost desperate hug.

Patricia froze for a heartbeat, startled by the suddenness of the gesture, then melted into it. She held the woman firmly, protectively, as though she could transfer her strength through the embrace. The woman's body trembled against hers, and Patricia felt the jagged rhythm of her breath, the silent sobs she was holding back.

"Thank you," the woman choked out, her voice breaking. "Thank you so very, very much."

Patricia blinked back the sting of tears. "You don't have to thank me," she said. "You deserve safety. You deserve peace. And you'll find both here. I promise."

The woman pulled back, her hands lingering on Patricia's arms for a moment before she let them fall. There was a flicker of something in her expression—hope, maybe, or just relief—but it was enough to make Patricia's chest ache.

"I'm glad to be of help," Patricia said, managing a small smile. "You'll be safe here. And you can stay as long as you need. These are good people."

The woman nodded, clutching her bag to her chest as if it were a lifeline. A volunteer appeared at her side, a soft-spoken young man with an easy smile, and motioned for her to follow.

"You're in good hands," Patricia assured her, stepping back to give her space.

The woman lingered for a moment, her gaze flicking to Patricia one last time. Then, with a small nod, she turned and followed the volunteer down the hall.

Patricia watched her go, a mix of relief and sadness settling over her. She couldn't save everyone, but for this one woman, for this one moment, she had made a difference. Patricia turned back toward the lobby door, ready to face whatever the next rescue might bring.

Outside, she stopped on the shelter's worn steps, her eyes scanning. People. Vehicles. Windows. Doors. Cameras. No threats apparent.

She slipped on sunglasses. The Spanish moss on the centuries-old oaks across from her swayed in the light breeze. The run-down porches on either side of the shelter were already decked out with simple Thanksgiving swag. The clip-clop of a horse-drawn carriage with a family of four and a tour guide drew her attention. Even though the summer tourist throng was gone, a trickle remained.

Fall in Savannah was one of her favorite seasons. The heat and humidity of summer was gone. And November, following on the heels of Halloween, was a joyous time of house parties, galas, and, of course, Thanksgiving, which meant her daughter, Hayley, would come home from college. They spoke daily, but this would be the first time Hayley would be home since the semester began.

The rescue had provided an intense morning, and as usual, it would be a busy day overall. With the cooler nights coming, she needed to put out the heated house for the feral cats. And it was well past time to replace her Halloween decorations with Thanksgiving items.

On the way home, she picked up her gown and Trey's tux from the dry cleaners. The next gala was just a couple of days away. She enjoyed big events where she could visit with so many acquaintances, but also harbored persistent fears for Trey's safety in such unsecure settings. Nothing had ever happened at the special events they attended, but his controversial cases and long list of serious enemies had both of them conscious of their surroundings at all times. Vigilance was a way of life for them-she looked to her purse and so was concealed carry.

Patricia stopped by the Falcon Hospital for a short meeting, then headed home.

She was rearranging the delicate, heirloom Thanksgiving swag on her mantel when her cell chimed. *Isabel Alton.* Patricia paused, trying to recall if she had any unfinished legal business with her attorney. None came to mind.

Suddenly, Patricia's breath caught. Had something happened to Isabel's father? Lucius had been battling stage-four cancer for almost a year.

"Hello, Isabel," Patricia said. "How are you?"

"Not well." Isabel's voice sounded strained.

Patricia stiffened. Isabel was normally a paragon of emotional stability. "Oh. I'm *so* sorry. Is… is Lucius okay?"

"He's well." Isabel sniffed. "I'd rather talk in person, Patricia. I know it's short notice, but could you come over?"

"Of course," Patricia said filled with concern for Isabel and her father.

"My house. Not my office."

Except for social events, Isabel, a very private person, never saw anyone at home. And the urgency in Isabel's voice spoke volumes. This was not to be a social visit.

"I'll be right over."

CHAPTER 2

*I*t was raining when Patricia parked her Navigator in front of Isabel's home, one of the many meticulously restored houses in Savannah's acclaimed historic district. Patricia knew very well Savannah's historic beauty was a velvet glove over an iron fist.

She stepped out of the SUV, popped an umbrella, and dashed up the wide stairs to the immense wrap-around front porch. Just as she closed the umbrella, one of the etched glass doors opened to reveal a somber-faced Isabel. Her gray hair was mostly pulled back, and she was dressed in tattered jeans and a loose, white T-shirt. Her face was void of makeup. Despite knowing Isabel for years, Patricia had never seen her dressed so casually or looking so disheveled.

Patricia's heart sank as she leaned the umbrella against the doorframe. She embraced Isabel, feeling tiny as she was enveloped by Isabel's tall and large-boned body.

"Thank you for coming over," Isabel said, sustaining the hug.

"Anytime." Patricia stroked her friend's back.

Isabel led Patricia to an elegant Victorian sitting room

just off the large foyer. A beautiful Tiffany chandelier provided illumination. Rain pounded on the floral chintz-draped windows.

Elizabeth, Isabel's housekeeper, appeared.

"Would you care for some tea?" Isabel asked.

"Yes. Please."

"My guest will have some PG Tips tea, please, Elizabeth."

Elizabeth left to fetch the tea.

Patricia gave Isabel a heartfelt smile. "Thank you for remembering my favorite brand."

"That's what friends do." Isabel gestured toward an antique settee covered with maroon brocade. They sat facing each other.

Elizabeth returned with tea and placed the silver service tray on a mahogany coffee table in front of them. Once Elizabeth left, Isabel served. The process seemed to settle her somewhat.

Patricia accepted the offered cup. "Thank you." She sipped tea and returned her cup to the saucer in tandem with Isabel. Then Patricia raised her eyebrows to encourage conversation.

Isabel took a folder from the end table beside her. "I think Lucius may have been conned by his oncologist into a shady deal that could kill him."

"Oh no. What kind of deal?"

Isabel handed the folder to Patricia. "I don't trust his doctor, Patricia. Look at those bills. Look at the doctor's notes. This doesn't add up."

Tension crackled like electrified air as Patricia flipped through the file.

"Clinical trials. Off-label prescriptions. And this… $50,000 for an experimental treatment? It does look suspicious."

"Magnum Oncology has been giving Lucius daily infusions for a month. And, apparently, they didn't work." Isabel's hazel eyes narrowed. "Totally useless and outrageously expensive."

"Perhaps it takes some time to produce results. Are his treatments done?"

"Yes. And because the infusions didn't work at all, they're switching him to another, even more expensive drug."

Patricia felt her eyebrows pinch together. "What about Medicare? Surely Medicare covers cancer treatments."

"Medicare and his private insurance said Magnum's treatments weren't FDA approved, so they didn't cover any of his previous infusions and won't cover the next round. Something about that doesn't seem right. I'd like you to check Magnum Oncology out."

"I must be honest with you, Isabel. This sounds like a conversation you should be having with the police and the Georgia Medical Board." Patricia set the folder aside.

"Maybe later. When I have evidence."

"I don't know anything about medical fraud. Why don't you use the Cotton Coalition to investigate Magnum? You're the head of the Coalition. They may be secretive, but they have far more resources and contacts than I do. Isn't this kind of thing what they're here to do?"

Isabel seemed to bow over the weight of her worry. "That's a good suggestion. We do have great lawyers, like your husband, and excellent doctors, like Beau. However, if the Cotton Coalition got involved, my father would certainly find out," Isabel said with a slight hint of disapproval. "Until I'm certain Magnum is running a scam, I don't want my father to know about the investigation. If he found out, he'd go ballistic. He thinks Dr. Gryoti is a medical genius. It's common knowledge that a patient's confidence in his doctor greatly affects his attitude, and a positive attitude has been shown to increase the odds of whipping cancer. Dad can't know until we're sure. That's why I called you."

Patricia shrugged. "I don't know."

Isabel reached over and touched Patricia's arm. "Please help. You're all I have."

Patricia's will melted like butter in a hot pan. "Okay. I appreciate your faith in me." Patricia straightened. "What else do you have on Magnum?"

"Just suspicions. I'm not certain anything is wrong. In fact, I'd be delighted if you determined they were totally legitimate. But the information about the clinic on the internet is spotty, insurance said the infusions weren't FDA approved, my father's treatments didn't work, and so I'm suspicious."

"Are you sure you want to do this? If I find Magnum is committing fraud, it will take that glimmer of hope from your father."

"He's a reasonable man, and he's dying. He's running out of time. He can't afford to waste another week much less a month on ineffective treatments."

Patricia took Isabel's hand. "Anything else?"

"Please be very discreet in your work, Patricia. I don't want even a hint of this to get back to my father."

"I understand." Patricia leaned in and gave Isabel a hug, weaving them together in warmth. "By the way, would you and Lucius like to join me and Trey for the Thanksgiving buffet at the Hyatt?"

Isabel leaned back, pinched the bridge of her nose, then looked up. "I'd love to, Patricia, but with all the treatments Dad is highly vulnerable to infection. So we don't go out. Doctor's orders." Isabel stood. "I've arranged catering for Thanksgiving but thank you so much for thinking of us."

Patricia put the folder in her purse, stood, and walked with Isabel to the door.

"Thank you for your help and understanding," Isabel said.

"Twenty years of friendship, Isabel. We'll figure this one out just like we always have."

PATRICIA SAT IN HER NAVIGATOR FOR A MOMENT BEFORE starting the engine. She loved investigation, but even more, she took great pride in turning a solid case over to the authorities. This one was different though. Poor Lucius. If he was simply the recipient of bad luck that his treatments didn't work, that would be one thing. But to think Lucius could be the target of some unscrupulous charlatan cashing in on a dying man's last hope made her blood boil.

She didn't have a clue how to go about investigating possible medical fraud. Where to start? Well, she'd learned long ago to call in experts when she was out of her element. And the best physician-actually ex-physician-she knew was the one Isabel had already mentioned-Beau Simpson. He was a close friend of hers, but he was also close with Lucius. Could she trust Beau to remain discrete if she reached out to him? She certainly hoped so, but to be certain, she'd keep Lucius's name out of her initial conversation. Patricia called Beau and arranged to see him on her way home.

Ten minutes later, Patricia parked in the public garage across the street from Beau's new employer, a printing company. She took the elevator to ground level, crossed the street, and entered the stark commercial building, where she identified herself to a gruff security guard.

Moments later, a young lady came into the lobby. "Mr. Simpson will see you now."

Patricia followed the woman down a dingy linoleum-tiled hall to the entrance to Beau's office where the lady gestured Patricia to enter. She stepped into a sparsely furnished, harshly lit office.

Beau, dressed in khakis and a short-sleeved white shirt, stood in front of a simple steel desk that had seen better days. His sheer height—a towering six feet eight inches—momentarily eclipsed her thoughts. His long brown hair framed a face so striking it seemed almost sculpted: wide, tapered chin, gold-flecked dark eyes, and eyebrows so perfect they felt at odds with his rugged presence. He looked heavier and harder than the last time she'd seen him, no doubt the result of his year in prison. His dark-brown hair was even longer than she remembered.

"So nice of you to stop by." Beau extended his hand.

After shaking Patricia's hand, he led her to a small conference table and held her chair while she sat. Always the gentleman.

"How have you been, Beau?" Patricia asked.

He nodded slowly. "I'm doing okay. Thanks to Trey and the Coalition, I landed a well-paying product management job here. It's not where I'd like to be ultimately, practicing again, but it pays the bills while I try to get my license back. How are you doing?"

"Empty nesting has been a challenge, but we're doing well."

Beau stroked his wide, tapered chin. "So. What can I do for you, Patricia?"

"Magnum Oncology. What do you know about them?"

"Dr. Gryoti is a reputable oncologist. If I had cancer, I wouldn't hesitate to go to him. He has an outstanding medical education and is board certified. Also, he's been at the forefront of several promising cancer treatments, and in lieu of traditional treatments, I'm told he offers many of his patients the opportunity to participate in clinical trials of some drugs he deems appropriate for them."

Beau paused, focusing on his hands, now resting on the table. "It's scientifically responsible to conduct carefully controlled human trials of experimental drugs, but there is no real scientific evidence that those drugs in his trials are effective or totally safe. That's why all the subjects must volunteer to participate in the trials, and those who participate are closely monitored."

Patricia showed Beau a Magnum Oncology advertisement from the folder Isabel had provided. "What do you think of this ad?"

Beau's brow furrowed as he scanned the photocopy. "I wouldn't advertise that way, if I advertised at all."

"What specifically don't you like about the ad?"

Beau looked more closely at the copy. "It's retailing medicine. It's claiming to be the best cancer center, which is fine if that's what they believe, but it's also falsely claiming to get results others don't get. Guaranteed results. Drug results can't be guaranteed. There are far too many variables. I definitely think the ad is misleading."

"But the ad works?"

Beau nodded. "I've heard Magnum Oncology has all the business they can handle and are recruiting additional oncologists. So it is definitely working to get more prospective patients through the door."

"Why doesn't Medicare cover Magnum's treatments?"

Beau eyes widened. "Medicare should cover FDA approved treatments that are medically indicated and prescribed by a licensed doctor. But typically, people involved in clinical trials are only charged for the doctor's time, if even that, not the drugs. What's going on, Patricia?"

Patricia wished she could tell Beau everything, but she'd promised Isabel she'd keep her investigation discrete. "A friend of mine was treated unsuccessfully at Magnum, and neither his Medicare nor private insurance covered the infusions nor a proposed additional treatment."

"Typically they won't pay if the meds aren't FDA

approved, or if they don't feel the medication is necessary even if it is FDA approved."

"Magnum's infusions didn't help my friend." Patricia leaned forward. "Do you think my friend's situation could be classified as medical fraud?"

"I'm not a lawyer, so you should talk with Trey about the legal aspects of what constitutes fraud. From a physician's standpoint, I could be guilty of fraud if I knowingly mislead a patient about the effectiveness of a treatment or a drug." Beau pointed to the ad photocopy. "And I'd certainly be guilty if the patient relied on my false statements, and I charged them for the treatment." Beau took a breath. "However, the courts have held that if I sugar-coat or puff up a treatment that's not fraud if my statements are only minor misrepresentations. In addition, to be fraudulent the misrepresentations must have been a significant factor in the patient's decision to participate in the treatment or use the drug."

"This sounds quite technical," Patricia said.

Beau shrugged. "It can be. But it can also be pretty simple. Back in 2019, a California physician was indicted for selling a pineapple extract as a cancer cure despite the lack of any clinical trials proving the claim. Whether or not it worked was moot."

"So the key point is whether or not the treatment has been FDA approved so everyone knows it may work on most people, even if not necessarily all?"

Beau nodded. "The only exception to that is for patients participating in clinical trials. In that case, the treatment is, by definition, unproven. To protect themselves, after a physician discusses voluntary participation in a clinical trial with a patient, they generally have the patient sign an informed consent form that fully describes the risks and benefits and the terms of the patient's participation."

"How can I tell if a cancer treatment has been proven to work?"

"The National Cancer Institute and others publish lists on the internet of the drugs approved by the FDA for specific types of cancer. They're searchable." Beau paused in thought. "Medical fraud investigations are complex. I have a friend who might help guide you further." Beau jotted a note and tore it from the tablet. "Ellery Hampton. She's a former DEA agent. She might be willing to help you frame a legal case against Gryoti." He handed the paper to Patricia. "This is her contact information."

"Thank you." Patricia put the note in her purse. "Is there anything else I should know?"

Beau's face tightened. "Just a warning to be careful. Big practices like Magnum don't take criticism lightly. If you go after them, they're likely to push back hard. And, if they are knowingly engaging in fraud, they'll probably hit you with everything they can. In a word, Patricia, investigating Magnum could be dangerous."

CHAPTER 3

*P*atricia met DEA agent Ellery Hampton in the lobby of the Gryphon Tea Room restaurant later that afternoon. Patricia extended her hand to the short, slender, smiling woman. "Thank you for meeting with me on such short notice."

"No problem." Ellery gave Patricia's hand a firm shake. "Any friend of Beau's is a friend of mine."

Patricia nodded as she scanned the restaurant for threats. It appeared clear, but one never knew for certain. She watched in silence as Ellery did the same. "Such a shame about Beau's difficulty," Patricia added.

"Yes indeed. I'm glad it's over, and he's starting a new life. He's a strong man."

Patricia wondered if there was more to their relationship than business.

A waiter showed them to an isolated table by the windows. Out of habit, Patricia sat with her back to a side wall and with a good line of sight of the front door, as well as the door to the kitchen.

The waiter took their order.

"So you worked with the DEA." Patricia studied the woman's face. A strong, determined face, framed with short gray hair.

"Yes. Almost thirty years."

"Do you miss it?"

"Yes and no. Mostly no." The engaging smile returned. "How can I help you?"

"A close friend asked me to look into a possible medical fraud, and I don't have a clue how to go about that. I asked Beau for advice, and he suggested you might be able to help me understand how to pursue the investigation."

Ellery's eyes narrowed. "Are you with the police?"

"No."

"Private investigator?"

"Not officially."

"What investigative experience do you have?"

"A murder. A kidnapping. A Ponzi scheme. And a bit of terrorism. I'm just a private citizen who tries to help my friends."

"That's very noble of you, but I must tell you upfront that proving medical fraud can be both time consuming and complex. And unlike your previous investigations where you had to identify a perpetrator, in this kind of case, the perpetrator is assumed. It's the crime you must prove."

Patricia reached for her purse. "Do you mind if I take notes?"

"Not at all."

While Patricia removed her notebook and pen, tea arrived and was served. Both had ordered Oolong, so they shared a pot. "Would you like something to eat?" Patricia asked.

"No, thank you. You?"

Patricia shook her head.

Ellery took a sip of tea, then returned the China cup to its saucer. "Tell me the specifics of who you're investigating and what evidence you have of fraud."

Feeling vulnerable, Patricia released a breath. "I don't even know if there is fraud. That's why I'm investigating. All I have to go on is that the medical treatments aren't working. The who is Magnum Oncology."

Ellery's smile disappeared. "Nothing like starting out at the top of the food chain. Despite Magnum's outstanding reputation, the DEA has long had unsubstantiated suspicions about their operations."

"Did you investigate them?"

"No. Not directly. We and the FDA asked the FBI to do an initial investigation."

"Where did that go?"

"Nowhere."

"Why?"

"Unfortunately, the lead agent died in an automobile accident. Due to the low priority of the investigation, it was shut down in favor of higher priority cases."

"How would you suggest I go about investigating Magnum?"

Ellery paused in thought for a moment. "Obviously, evidence is everything. Without admissible evidence, you don't have a case. You'll need two types of evidence. First, the composition of the drugs in question. Second, the claims being made about those drugs."

"How would I identify the drugs?"

"They might be listed in the patient's profile, but if they're fraudulent, they'll be obscured and information about them closely controlled. If that's the case, you'll need to get actual samples. The easiest way is to have someone inside provide them to you. But that involves finding a disgruntled employee or whistleblower which usually involves a lot of legwork. Beyond that, you'd have to use your imagination."

Patricia jotted notes, then looked up. "What about evidence of false claims being made?"

"Of course advertising should be examined, but experienced con men are usually very careful in that regard. Next would be false claims being made by the doctor in the course of discussions with a patient. And to avoid denials by the doctor, you would want to record them."

"Anything else?"

"Besides medical fraud, these kinds of cases often include insurance fraud, so checking Magnum's financial records for fraud is another avenue."

Patricia thought of her best friend Meredith, who seemed to be able to find financial records on anyone. "What would be my absolute first step?"

"Because you have no evidence yet, I suggest you do a preliminary assessment. This would involve identifying and gathering information from dissatisfied patients, whistleblowers, and other healthcare professionals. Unfortunately, you'll be surprised how unwilling most people are to complain about a well-regarded firm. And just because someone complains, it doesn't mean their information is actionable. Just keep digging until you find people who actually know what is going on inside Magnum. But be aware that companies engaging in fraud generally keep their information highly compartmentalized. So if you get some actionable information, don't assume it's the whole story. Keep digging until you've exhausted all your resources."

"This has been very helpful." Patricia returned her notebook to her purse. "Thank you so much."

"You're welcome." Ellery's face sobered. "Be careful. If Dr. Gryoti is committing fraud, he's not going to go down peacefully."

"I appreciate your warning."

The waiter appeared. "More tea?"

Patricia glanced at Ellery, who shook her head. Patricia turned to the waiter. "No. Just the check, please."

Ellery looked at her watch. "Anything else?"

Patricia paid the bill. "Can I get back to you if I have questions later?"

Ellery flashed a smile and pushed back her chair. "Of course."

CHAPTER 4

On arriving at the Alton Law office the following morning, Patricia was shown into Isabel's suite; the same office her father, Lucius, had occupied before his retirement. Isabel wore black slacks and a yellow silk blouse. Her gray hair was down in a short bob. No sign of yesterday's distress. After exchanging greetings, Isabel gestured toward a pair of highbacked leather chairs in one corner of the large, mahogany-paneled room.

"Thank you for seeing me on such short notice," Patricia said as she sat.

"How's the investigation going?" Isabel settled into the other chair, leaned back, and rested her hands over the ends of the armrests.

"Just feeling my way at this point. Which is why I asked to speak with you again."

Isabel nodded. "Anytime, Patricia. You know how important this is to me. Anytime at all."

"Here's the deal. You said Lucius's infusions didn't work, but I have no idea what drug he was being treated with. Do you?"

"No, not really."

"I'm going to need that information."

Isabel's fingertips traced the ends of the armrests. "I'll see what I can do. I don't think it's a secret, but I'm not certain my father knows. As far as I recall, we've never discussed the specific drugs he has received. His medical conversations are always focused on his admiration for Dr. Gryoti."

Patricia paused. "Magnum may have given your father some product literature or a patient datasheet on the infusion drug. If so, I need those as well."

"I'll have to be careful about being too inquisitive. His mind is still razor sharp, and he's likely to see through any subterfuge."

"You could say you're asking for a friend who is undergoing cancer treatment elsewhere."

Isabel let out a long breath. "I hate to lie to him. I'll find a way, Patricia. Anything else?"

"Do you have access to your father's patient portal?"

"No." Isabel's thick brows pinched. "Why?"

"It could be a treasure trove of information. And it's probably a good idea for you to have access in the event of, heaven forbid, something happening to him. I assume you're his next of kin?"

"I am."

Patricia recalled how unprepared she had been when her mother died. Painful memories surged. Memories of a sweet life taken too soon. "I think it would be a good idea for you two to discuss you having access to all of his medical records in order to make informed decisions in case things go downhill fast. And you probably should consider getting a medical power of attorney as well."

"Good idea." Isabel keyed a note into her phone. "What information do you want from his patient portal?"

"For starters, I'd like full details of his infusions. Treatment code. Treatment drug. Dose. Treatment dates. Also, specifically what type of cancer Dr. Gryoti is treating him for.

"You should also ask Lucius to give all his providers permission to share information with you so they can speak freely with you if things deteriorate. It's a hard conversation, Isabel, but you must do it. Not for me. Not for the investigation. But for you. And, most importantly, for Lucius. It's best to be prepared."

Isabel keyed a few more notes, then put her phone down. "We've been putting off that discussion, but you're right, we need to get it done. And I'll do it today."

"When you get access to his medical records, it could be overwhelming. Focus first on identifying all the drugs he's been given and in what order. Once I get that, I can find out if the drugs are FDA approved for his type of cancer. Second, see if there is any record of Lucius participating in any clinical trials at Magnum. If yes, look for informed consent agreements."

"Oh geez." Isabel stiffened. "I hadn't even considered he might have signed hold harmless agreements for the drugs. That would certainly complicate matters."

"Or uncomplicate them," Patricia said, registering the disappointment in Isabel's voice. "But a lot depends on how Dr. Gryoti represented the drugs he has given to your father."

"Well, Father *is* a careful man and an excellent lawyer. He would have read any agreement Gryoti asked him to sign. Especially a hold harmless agreement."

"I sure hope so."

"You've certainly given me a lot to work on."

"If you can only do one thing, get me the names of the drugs."

Isabel smiled. "I'll do better than that. I'll get it all."

Patricia returned the smile. "You always do."

Once Patricia got home, she had a small salad for lunch, then checked the FDA website to see if Dr. Gryoti was an FDA-approved clinical investigator and learned he wasn't. Then she searched the National Institutes of Health clinical trial database to see if the doctor was listed as an investigator on any of the trials and came up empty. That didn't mean he couldn't do experimental or off-label studies, simply that his work wasn't yet on track for FDA approval.

Disappointed at the lack of any results on the clinical trial approach, she set up a case file, entered the information she already had, and continued online research on Dr. Gryoti. When she searched Google, she quickly located Demetrius Gryoti of Savannah. He had seventeen reviews with an average of 3.4 stars out of 5. Two of the reviews were one star, one of which started out, "Stay away from this quack. His drugs don't work." Patricia made a note of the reviewer's full name, intending to track her down later for a face-to-face interview. Same thing with the second one-star reviewer. And since she was maintaining an open mind, she read the five-star reviews and noted several of those reviewers for follow-up as well.

Since she still had a few hours before she had to get ready for the evening's gala, Patricia searched *healthgrades.com* as well, found Dr. Gryoti's education, board certifications, and awards, and recorded the information in her case file profile for him. Searching WebMD and *vitals.com* confirmed the information and added details. At each website there were both negative reviews, mostly complaining about poor outcomes, and glowing positive reviews. Unfortunately, it was impossible for Patricia to identify the reviewers on those sites.

Miffed at not being able to harvest more dissatisfied patients to interview, she went to Magnum Oncology's website to examine the information presented about Gryoti. According to the website, he was a graduate of Boston University School of Medicine and had done a residency at Memorial Sloan Kettering Cancer Center. His research training included being a research associate at Emerald University early in his career doing work in experimental oncology. He listed a two-year stint with the Cleveland Clinic and three years at the University of Georgia's School of Medicine. A few years later, he became chief of the Oncology Section at Emerald's Department of Medicine. Patricia made a note to identify the people he'd worked with at Emerald.

Patricia scoured the website for false claims and found nothing obvious. But in the *About* section she did find:

All cancers are different. All patients respond differently to treatment. To effectively treat patients, Dr. Gryoti personalizes his treatment for each patient.

So there it was; a claim to *effectively* treat patients. Now she needed evidence to prove that claim was false.

She did a background check and found several DUIs spread over a couple of decades and a slew of unsuccessful malpractice claims. She made a note to check with the attorneys representing the plaintiffs. No telling what evidence they possessed.

Gryoti also had a disciplinary action and state sanction during his residency for conducting a human trial of an experimental drug without approval from Sloan Kettering's Institutional Review Board. She made a note of those items.

She checked his medical license status at the Georgia Composite Medical Board and found the current license had two more years before he had to renew it. As she scrolled down Gryoti's profile, she saw no disciplinary actions, no hospital privilege revocations, no criminal offenses, and no medical malpractice awards. She wondered why the sanction at Sloan Kettering hadn't been listed on his Georgia license profile and guessed he might have changed states to hide that fact.

The extensive profile also listed eight articles he'd authored over the past ten years, including two on novel cancer treatments and one on evidence-based medicine in esophageal cancer. There was a long list of awards, and a list of appointments to medical school faculties that confirmed the information she'd previously obtained and added that he was a peer reviewer for clinical breast cancer and esophageal cancer.

After recording all the information in her case file, she searched local newspaper archives for articles on Magnum Oncology and Gryoti. Only one article appeared. It was a piece written by her friend Willie Maye, an investigative reporter for the *Savannah Post*, five years previously reporting that the FBI had launched an investigation into Magnum Oncology for dispensing a non-approved drug. Her pulse quickened as she read the short article. For a second time, Gryoti appeared to be accused of conducting a drug trial on humans without proper approvals. She wondered what became of the investigation. As far as she could tell, Gryoti hadn't been sanctioned for that incident.

Patricia checked the clock. It wasn't quite time to start getting ready for the gala, so she called her friend Algenon Melfive, Resident Agent in Charge for Savannah's FBI office.

"How are you doing, Patricia?" he asked.

"Doing fine. And you?"

Algenon cleared his throat. "Things have been pretty quiet."

"Do you still have those Chinese agents under

surveillance?" she asked, referencing a previous investigation they'd collaborated on.

"Like cockroaches, they're always here, but we've been able to keep them from causing too many problems."

"That's great, Algenon. I called because I have a question about an investigation your office reportedly opened five years ago. Dr. Gryoti of Magnum Oncology. Ring a bell?"

She heard Algenon expel a long breath. "Afraid so. I know it well. The investigation never got off the ground. The lead investigator, Pete Dorsey, was killed in an automobile accident not long after he took the case. Such a tragic loss. He had four children."

"I'm so sorry." Patricia jotted down the agent's name.

"He was a rising star. They don't make many like him. And losing him cut into our manpower, so we abandoned the case."

"Did you investigate the auto accident?"

"No. But I'm sure the Chatham Police did."

Patricia made a note to check with the Chatham Police. "Why did the FBI open an investigation into Dr. Gryoti?"

"If I recall correctly, the FDA asked us. Let me check." There was a pause. "Okay. I have the case file. Let's see. Hmm. Two years before we opened the case, the FDA sent Gryoti a letter telling him he could no longer sell or conduct a trial of an unapproved cancer drug. They sent a second letter a year later. He ignored both, so the FDA involved us."

"What was the name of the drug?"

"Blanscan. It's a sassafras extract. No known effect on cancer"

Patricia made a note of the name. "Thank you, Algenon."

"Any time."

Patricia knew she should start getting ready for the gala, but another five minutes wouldn't set her far behind. She called Willie Maye.

"Well, well, well," Willie exclaimed. "Patricia Falcon. My favorite amateur sleuth."

"Good afternoon, Willie. Do you have a minute?"

"For you, always. What do you need?"

"You wrote a piece five years ago about the FBI opening an investigation of Magnum Oncology."

"I don't recall, but I'll take your word for it. What do you want to know?"

"Details."

"Hold on," he said. She heard clicking of computer keys. "Here it is." There was a pause. "Okay. I remember now. The FBI was just beginning their investigation of Magnum Oncology when their lead investigator was killed. I think it was an automobile accident. They dropped the case after his death. Not enough manpower."

"I know you, Willie. You don't drop cases. What happened to *your* investigation?"

"I continued to look into Magnum's activities until they got wind of my investigation and threatened the paper with a lawsuit. We don't have deep pockets, so my editor told me to stand down. I was a bit spooked and didn't want to drop it, but the investigation went cold on me."

"Do you recall the name of the non-approved drug?"

"Not offhand, but I may have it in my notes. I'll check."

"If you find it, let me know. And, Willie, in your opinion, was Magnum guilty of dispensing a non-approved drug?"

"My gut, which rarely fails me, said yes, but I couldn't prove it."

On completing the very informative call with Willie, Patricia checked the time-three. It had been an intriguing day of investigating, but Trey would be home in a couple of hours. She had to get ready for the gala.

CHAPTER 5

*P*atricia was applying the last of her makeup when Trey came into the dressing room and gave her a cheek kiss. "How was your day?" she asked.

"Fine," he said as he removed his jacket and tie. "And yours?"

"I've taken on a new case."

He unbuttoned his cuffs and started on the front of his shirt. "What are you investigating this time?"

She put away her makeup and turned to face him. "Possible medical fraud."

Trey dumped his shirt in the wicker laundry basket, then unbuckled his belt. "Who's the target?"

"Magnum Oncology."

"I've heard they're the local go-to clinic for anyone with cancer. In fact, people travel from all over the country to be treated there. And they run a free cancer clinic for the underserved in Savannah. Why do you think there may be fraud?"

Patricia removed a black sequined clutch from the shelf and, after checking the chamber and magazine, put a compact handgun into her purse along with the rest of her essentials. "I don't know for certain there's fraud, but a good friend of ours asked me to look into it."

"Who?" Trey asked as he stepped into the bathroom.

Patricia followed him into the bathroom. "Trey, honey," she said, softening her voice. "What I'm about to tell you is absolutely confidential."

Trey turned and nodded his acknowledgement.

"Isabel Alton asked me to look into treatments Lucius is receiving at Magnum."

"His eyes widened. "What? Why?"

"Medicare wouldn't cover his current treatment there, and now that it's done and didn't work, the clinic is proposing a totally different treatment."

"That's how medicine goes. Sometimes it works. Sometimes it doesn't. Why does Lucius think his last treatment was fraudulent?"

"According to Isabel, he doesn't. He thinks his oncologist is a miracle worker."

Trey applied shaving cream, then swiped the left side of his face with his razor. "Then why—"

"It's Isabel who's skeptical."

Trey finished shaving the right side and started on the left. "Does she have a reason for her skepticism beyond the treatment not working?"

"Other than Medicare not approving the treatment, no."

"Knowing Lucius, he wouldn't have chosen Magnum unless they were reputable. Sounds like a wild-goose chase." He tilted his face to reach his neck.

"Perhaps. But she's a good friend. For her peace of mind, I said yes." Patricia paused and took a deep breath. "And I did something else."

Trey stopped shaving and stared at her with eyebrows lifted.

"At Isabel's request, I promised Lucius wouldn't find out about my investigation."

Trey turned on the shower. "So I have to sit on this information?"

"Afraid so."

Trey resumed shaving. "Okay. But the same way you and I are completely open with each other, I'm open with Lucius. You're asking me to mislead him. It's going to kill me to keep this from him."

Patricia winced. "I'm sorry. It's only until I know for sure whether there's fraud."

"Okay," he said as he rinsed his razor and put it away. "But not a moment longer."

* * *

PATRICIA AND TREY ARRIVED AT THE SAVANNAH BAR Association's Black and White Gala at six thirty. A white-gloved valet opened her door, and she picked up the hem of her black formal and stepped out of the Bentley.

Trey came around the car and took her arm. "You look wonderful tonight."

They walked the red carpet into the venue, a restored roundhouse dating to 1853. Chitchatting lawyers and their guests gathered throughout the spacious room that had been transformed into a glitzy ballroom. An eight-piece band played up-tempo music while servers circulated with silver trays of champagne and a wide variety of canapes. Over-the-top white floral centerpieces dominated each of the eight-person tables. It was an important annual gala and sure to raise a lot of money for a slew of local charities.

Patricia grabbed a flute of champagne from the tray offered by a young server and, on Trey's arm, moved to a small circle of people she and Trey knew.

"What have you been up to?" she asked Louisa, the wife of Collin Patrick, Savannah's Chief of Police.

The dark-haired woman was about the same age as Patricia, looked pretty in her silver-sequined gown, and was ten years younger than her gray-haired, esteemed husband. "The law school is flourishing." As a trustee of the Savannah Law School, Louisa had every reason to be proud. They chatted about the school for several minutes.

Patricia spotted Meredith Stanwick, her best friend and banker. Patricia stepped back. "It's so nice to have spoken with you, Louisa. I hope you have a wonderful evening."

On the way to greet Meredith, Patricia did a quick scan of the attendees and almost stumbled as she recognized a face she'd only just learned to pay attention to-Dr. Gryoti. She recognized him from his omnipresent magazine and television ads. Nothing she'd discovered so far indicated he was married, but he seemed to be accompanied by an exceptionally attractive woman who complemented his handsomeness.

Patricia knew she'd build a relationship map on Gryoti, so she surreptitiously took a zoomed-in photo of Gryoti and his companion. She'd run it through facial recognition in the event she couldn't find someone at the gala who knew the woman's name. Then she took a second photo of the group of people Gryoti was speaking with. She recognized most of them and, over the next few days, would try to speak with each to get their impressions of Gryoti.

Patricia reached Meredith and the two embraced warmly. Patricia stepped back and eyed Meredith appreciatively, taking in her floor-length, white satin evening dress. "My but you look stunning tonight."

Meredith smiled. "Aww. Thank you, Patricia. You're so sweet and also stunningly alluring."

Patricia smiled. "How's your day been?"

"Other than an unannounced audit of my bank, it's been quite pleasant. How about yours?"

Patricia knew Meredith barely tolerated audits. "Nothing as dramatic as yours." She subtly gestured toward the Gryoti group. "Isn't that Dr. Gryoti?"

Meredith nodded. "We're fortunate to have him in our community. He's quite an asset. He's saved a lot of lives with his leading-edge cancer treatments. People travel from everywhere to be treated by him."

Patricia raised an eyebrow. "A friend asked me to look into him, so I'm kind of curious. Is he one of your depositors?"

"Maybe someday. I'm told he uses an offshore bank. I think it's in the Bahamas. Big income. Small expenses. A sizable one-way flow into that foreign bank."

"Small expenses? What about the cost of his TV ads? I see them all the time."

Meredith gave a nod. "They might be his biggest expense. That and the cancer drugs he uses. Anyway, still big income and proportionately smaller expenses."

"The woman Gryoti is with is certainly attractive. Is that his wife?"

"No. He's not married, but she's been with him at all the parties I've attended lately. I think her name is Carol something. From Atlanta. Moved here a year or so ago if I remember correctly. Very private. I've heard they live together."

"Engaged?"

"I don't think so. He's been in Savannah for at least five years, maybe more, and he seems to get a new girlfriend every year or so."

"Has he dated any locals?"

Meredith tilted her head. "What angle are you investigating, business or personal?"

"Both."

"What did he do to warrant an investigation?"

"Don't know yet."

Meredith raised her eyebrows. "Just allegations?"

"Exactly."

"Let me know if you need any help."

The band quieted and the president of the bar association took the stage. He welcomed the attendees and invited everyone to be seated for dinner.

On Patricia's way to their table, she stopped and pretended to take pictures of the event, while actually taking more photos of Gryoti and his girlfriend Carol. This time, the good doctor was mixing with a different group of people.

A pianist started playing quiet dinner music.

Patricia found her table, introduced herself to her table-mates, and sat.

To her right was Chief Patrick and his wife. To Trey's left was the CEO of the Savannah Design Academy and her husband. Across the table from Patricia was the Commander of the First Ranger Battalion at Hunter Army Airfield and his wife.

A server offered a choice of wine and Patricia selected chardonnay. A poached pear salad was already plated at each place setting.

"This pear is delicious," Chief Patrick said to her.

Patricia glanced at the menu, noting the pear had been poached in port. "It sure is."

"Detective Rodriquez asked me to pass his greetings to you tonight."

"Thank you. How is he doing?" Patricia put a piece of pear into her mouth and savored the decadent flavors.

"He's doing well. Fully recovered."

"That's wonderful. What is he up to?"

"Tracking several mainland Chinese gangsters who've recently taken up residence here."

"I thought y'all shut down that activity a year ago."

Chief Patrick nodded. "We did. Unfortunately, they're back. Apparently, they're serious about being here permanently. That's no problem as long as they obey our laws."

"Bad actors?"

Chief Patrick smiled. "Very bad."

"If I can help in any way, please let me know."

The Chief looked toward the stage. "That piano music is nice."

"That's Naomi Gryoti," Louisa Patrick said.

Patricia almost choked on her wine.

"She's Dr. Gryoti's daughter," Louisa continued. "A few years ago, she finaled in the Hilton Head International Piano Competition. I think she lives in New York. We're so fortunate to have her performing tonight."

Patricia nodded. "I'm sure Dr. Gryoti is proud of her accomplishments."

Louisa smiled. "He dotes on her."

CHAPTER 6

Patricia didn't sleep well that night. Her mind kept mulling Magnum's activities, wondering what Willie had done that angered Gryoti so much and what Willie had found that made him so certain the company was involved in fraud. She'd call him later in the morning and set up a face-to-face meeting.

Patricia climbed out of bed when Trey got up, made the bed, and went downstairs. After feeding the feral cats, she brought in the morning paper and made coffee.

Trey, dressed in a gray suit that matched the gray highlights of his hair, came into the kitchen and poured himself coffee. "You're up early."

Patricia, seated at the table in her robe, took a sip of coffee. "Sheila's coming over first thing with pumpkins for the porch and a new bouquet for the foyer."

"I can't wait to see what she comes up with." Trey put his coffee on the table, sat, and picked up the newspaper.

After Trey finished his coffee, she walked him to the back door, where they kissed, and he left for the garage. Patricia straightened the kitchen, went back upstairs, and changed into yoga pants and a tank top. She ran six miles on the treadmill, showered, and dressed. Moments after returning to the kitchen with her laptop, the front door chimed. Patricia glanced at the microwave clock. Sheila was early. Very early. Patricia went to the front door and checked the security screen. *Willie.* Why was he at her front door? And so early in the day. She opened the door.

Willie, dressed in navy blazer, white open-collar shirt, and gray slacks, had a big smile on his weathered face. "Sorry to bother you so early, Patricia," he said graciously.

She pushed back the long blonde tendrils in her face and tucked them behind her ears. "Good morning, Willie. So nice to see you. Would you care to join me for some coffee?"

Willie remained at the doorway. "That's very nice of you, but I'll just be a moment." He extended his hand, offering her a thumb drive. "I think you'll find this interesting."

Patricia took the drive. "What's on this?"

"A copy of my investigative files on Magnum Oncology."

Patricia inhaled deeply, then exhaled slowly. "That is considerate of you to share this." She clutched the drive to her chest. "Thank you so much. I was planning to call you later to ask what you found that convinced you Magnum was engaged in fraud."

"It's all in the files, and a lot more." Willie ran a hand through his longish ginger hair. "Let me know if you still have questions after you look it over."

Patricia held up the drive. "Thank you, Willie."

Willie nodded. "If you find anything interesting in your investigation, don't forget who gave you this information." He winked. "Good day, Patricia."

Patricia returned to the kitchen, opened a bag of candy corn, and poured some in a small bowl, which she placed on the kitchen table next to her laptop. She put her cold coffee in the microwave to warm it up.

While she waited for the coffee to heat, she grabbed a couple pieces of candy corn and went to the patio door to watch the two feral cats sleeping on their backs on the lawn in the morning sun. They seemed to be relaxed and at peace with the world, but she knew better. Feral cats were *always* vigilant and those two were no exception.

The microwave dinged. She removed her hot coffee, sat, and booted up her laptop. Once all was ready, she inserted the thumb drive and brought up Willie's files. Willie certainly had plenty of material from the looks of it, mostly notes from interviews. Since the material was organized chronologically, she decided to scan through it in that fashion to get a general feeling for what was there.

The first document contained notes from a confidential informant at the FBI, who advised Willie the local office was opening an investigation of Magnum Oncology over their use of a non-FDA approved drug. The informant mentioned Pete Dorsey was assigned the case.

She'd always believed Willie had an army of well-placed tipsters. There was no other explanation for his uncanny ability to get the big stories fast.

The second document was notes from a brief call to Pete Dorsey, who wouldn't discuss the case with Willie. The third document was a Freedom of Information request to the FDA for information on any and all FDA interactions with Magnum Oncology or any of their employees. All three documents were from the same day.

There was a letter to Willie from an Emerald University lawyer stating that any alleged work by Gryoti at the school was *not associated with any clinical privileges or with participation in any formal training here. Gryoti's use of his past association with us to provide credibility for his clinical practice can best be characterized as an inappropriate exaggeration.*

When Willie checked Gryoti's claim of working at the

UGA School of Medicine, the school had replied, *we are unable to verify Dr. Gryoti's claim to have been employed at our School of Medicine. To claim differently is a fraudulent credential.*

And, as to working at the Cleveland Clinic, the hospital replied, *we are unable to find any record of Dr. Gryoti being on our clinical staff.*

Apparently, at least some of Gryoti's claimed credentials were unsubstantiated. But was claiming false credentials illegal? Patricia made a note to check with Ellery Hampton.

Just as Patricia opened the next document in Willie's file, the front door chime sounded. A glance at the clock at the top of her laptop confirmed it was the time Sheila had said she'd be by with the monthly floral arrangement.

Patricia went to the foyer and opened one of the double doors to find Sheila carrying a large floral bouquet in autumn colors. Lots of mums. Some pussy willows. Beautiful, dried leaves. After a quick greeting, Patricia removed the old bouquet from the foyer table-a family heirloom with a hidden compartment containing a shotgun.

Sheila positioned the new arrangement on the table, took the old flowers from Patricia and returned to her van.

Meanwhile, Sheila's young assistant had begun to haul pumpkins from the van to the porch steps. One by one, step by step, the display took shape. Simple, but oh so festive.

Sheila returned from her van carrying several dried corn stalks. Her helper followed with more stalks.

"Those pumpkins are perfect," Patricia said. "And the new foyer arrangement is outstanding."

"I'm so glad you like them," Sheila said as she arranged the corn stalks in a tower on either side of the front doors.

Patricia's mind went to the abused women at the shelter who wouldn't have a festive Thanksgiving. "Are you doing anything at the shelter this fall?"

"We have an order for a Christmas tree, but we haven't received a Thanksgiving order."

"Please make sure each resident gets a nice arrangement in their room for Thanksgiving and put them on my bill."

Sheila's lips curled into a smile. "Bless you, Patricia."

Patricia couldn't ask for a more fulfilling activity than working with her team to rescue abused women. And she took much pride in supporting her decreased mother's shelter in any way possible.

Once Sheila and her helper left, Patricia returned to her laptop to review the next document in Willie's file, a copy of Gryoti's Chatham Police file showing several DUIs.

There was a note of an unattributed conversation in which Willie was told Gryoti had recently been sanctioned by the Georgia Composite Medical Board for practicing medicine while inebriated. There was also a Freedom of Information request to the Board for information on any sanctions of Gryoti.

Patricia continued scanning through the documents until she came to copies of the two research papers Gryoti had written years ago regarding experiments he'd conducted on holistic tumor treatments by indigenous healers. The first paper detailed the bioactivity of several herbal cures used by Oneida Indian medicine men. The principal finding was esophageal cancer tumor shrinkage in mice with a substance isolated from sassafras root. The second paper reported similar results in monkeys. Interestingly, the earlier information Patricia had found about Blanscan indicated it was basically a sassafras root extract.

So, Gryoti was exploring herbal remedies for cancer effectiveness. Nothing wrong with that as long as he went through the required trial steps before giving them to humans. Interesting, but not proof of fraud.

Patricia gave a resigned sigh and moved on to the next

document, a briefing paper on sassafras. The principle active ingredient in sassafras was safrole. Her eyes widened when she saw that safrole was an FDA identified carcinogen.

Geez. Wasn't sassafras used in making root beer and as a gumbo seasoning? Did Gryoti know that sassafras was carcinogenic when he was conducting his experiments? Had he given Blanscan to patients here in Savannah?

There was so much in Willie's files to sort out and make sense of, and she knew just who to discuss the situation with.

Summer Caldfield greeted Patricia at the front door of her Jones Street home, her latte-colored skin glowing softly in the lamplight. Her auburn hair, streaked with silver, was piled high in its signature messy bun, making her look both approachable and effortlessly elegant. She wore a simple navy-blue shift, and a delicate gold chain with a locket gleamed faintly against her collarbone.

Summer led Patricia down a hall, their heels clicking softly on the polished wooden floors. The house was warm and inviting, filled with soft light filtering through lace curtains. They entered a cozy sitting room. Bookshelves lined the walls, crammed with well-worn tomes on psychology, human behavior, and criminal profiling. A faint scent of jasmine tea lingered in the air.

"Patricia," Summer said in her gentle Southern drawl, her aquamarine eyes warm and understanding. She motioned to a plush armchair by the fireplace. "Sit down, darlin'. You look like you've got a world of worry on your shoulders."

Patricia smiled faintly, easing into the offered seat. "I do, Summer. And I think you're the only one who can help me figure some of it out."

Summer handed Patricia a cup of steaming jasmine tea before settling into the chair opposite her. She folded her fine-boned hands in her lap, the gold band of her wedding ring catching the light. "Tell me what's troubling you."

Patricia leaned forward, her voice low. "It's about Dr. Gryoti, the oncologist Isabel's father is seeing. There's something off about him—his treatments, his clinic, everything. I've been digging into his background, but I can't shake the feeling that he's manipulating everyone around him. The patients, his staff... maybe even the authorities."

Summer's brows knitted slightly, but her expression remained calm. "Tell me more about what you've found."

Patricia summarized the key points from her investigation so far: Gryoti's false credentials and the suspicious substances he was infusing patients with. As she spoke, Summer nodded thoughtfully, occasionally jotting notes in a leather-bound notebook.

When Patricia finished, Summer leaned back, her eyes narrowing slightly in focus. "Gryoti sounds like a textbook narcissist," she began. "These types thrive on control and adoration. He likely preys on his patients' desperation to make himself appear like a savior. The false credentials and secretive behavior suggest he's also deeply insecure—a house of cards he's fervently trying to keep from collapsing."

"How do I get through that?" Patricia asked. "How do I uncover the truth?"

"First, start by looking at the cracks in his facade. Someone that controlling always leaves a trail—disgruntled employees, patients who feel betrayed, staff who've seen more than they should. These are the people who can help you, but they're likely scared of him."

Patricia nodded.

Summer smiled faintly, her freckled face softening. "Build trust with them. Show them you're not just trying to expose Gryoti—you're trying to protect others from him. And if you can, find out what motivates Gryoti most. If you understand his deepest fear or desire, you'll know where to strike."

"Fear or desire?" Patricia echoed, tilting her head.

"For someone like him, it could be his reputation, his money, or even someone he cares about. Everyone has a weakness, Patricia. Find his, and you'll have the key to bringing him down."

Patricia's lips curved into a determined smile. "I knew you'd know how to help. Thank you, Summer."

Summer reached across the small table and placed her hand gently over Patricia's. "You're not alone in this, darlin'. Remember that. And if you need anything—even just someone to talk to—you know where to find me."

Patricia squeezed Summer's hand and nodded. "I do. And I will."

CHAPTER 7

Once Patricia returned home, she made the dough for a pie she'd finish later. While the dough chilled, she poured coffee and called Chief Patrick for the police report of the accident that killed FBI Agent Pete Dorsey five years previous.

"Hi, Collin," she said. "It was nice spending time with you last night."

"Likewise. What can I do for you?"

"There was a traffic accident five years ago that killed an FBI agent, Pete Dorsey. I'm doing an investigation that might have something to do with the agent. Could I, by any chance, get a copy of the accident report?"

"Of course. I'll have my secretary email it to you as soon as I hang up. Pete Dorsey, right?"

"Yes."

"If you don't mind me asking, what are you investigating?"

"I'm looking into the alleged fraudulent cancer treatment Dorsey was investigating for the FDA."

"What did Dorsey conclude?"

"Algenon said the investigation stalled with Dorsey's death. Insufficient manpower."

"Why resurrect it now after five years?"

"I think the alleged fraudulent treatment could be back on the market."

"Oh. Okay. Let me know if you need anything else."

"Will do."

Following her conversation with Chief Patrick, she set the oven to preheat. While the oven heated, Patricia reread her case file to build a new to-do list.

The more she read, the more she yawned. She hadn't slept well and was desperately in need of a nap, but she pressed on reviewing her case file for subjects to follow up on. She bunched her hair on top of her head with a scrunchy, took another piece of candy corn, and continued reading. Her eyelids drooped with fatigue. She popped another piece of candy and read on.

As soon as the email with the Dorsey accident report arrived, Patricia read through it. Basically, it was inconclusive. She exported the report to her case file for later follow-up.

Once her new to-do list was complete, Patricia rolled out the pie dough, put it into a pie pan, and set it in the preheated oven. While it was baking, Isabel called. Anticipation expanded in Patricia's chest.

"We missed you and Lucius at the Black and White Gala last night," Patricia said.

"Did you have a good time?"

"Yes indeed. Great dinner. Fabulous music. And the live auction was as spirited as ever." Patricia grabbed a couple pieces of candy corn. Those little sugar bombs were a life ring for her drowsiness.

"That's great," Isabel said. "While you were out partying, I spoke to Dad about giving me access to his medical records. He agreed it was time to do that. As a result, I was able to access his patient portal. He has received three drugs from Magnum. Blanscan, Stemase, and Dustare. I can't believe how expensive they were. Which would be okay if they worked, but they didn't."

Patricia jotted down the names of the three drugs. "Did your father receive any written information on the drugs?"

"Not that he recalls."

"Have you found any evidence that Lucius participated in any clinical trials at Magnum?"

"There was nothing about clinical trials in his patient portal, so I asked him directly. He told me Dr. Gryoti has never said a word about clinical trials."

"So, no hold harmless agreement."

"Not a trace," Isabel said. "That's all I have, Patricia."

"That's plenty."

"I hope it moves your investigation along."

"It does. Thank you."

After completing the call, Patricia removed the baked pie shell from the oven and set it aside to cool. Patricia checked the clock. *Three p.m.* Trey would be home in two hours, and she still had to order dinner and finish the sweet potato pie, Trey's favorite. She called The Olde Pink House and ordered two crispy flounder dinners for delivery at five thirty.

She made the sweet potato filling and set the mixer to slow. Once the mixture was smooth and the sugar dissolved, she spread the filling evenly in the pie shell and placed the pie in the oven.

While the pie baked, Patricia further researched Blanscan which she found on an FDA list of fake cancer cures consumers should avoid. She found no information at all on Stemase and Dustare.

An hour later, with the sweet smell of cinnamon in the air, she removed the pie and put it on the wire rack to cool, then made whipped cream for topping the pie when served.

Trey arrived home just after five, and they chatted about his day until dinner arrived at five-thirty.

As usual, the crispy flounder with apricot shallot sauce was superb, as were the grits and the collards.

"Dessert now or later?" Patricia asked as she cleared the dishes.

"What's for dessert?"

"Sweet potato pie."

Trey gave a warm smile. "Now, please."

She sliced him a large piece, a smaller one for herself, topped both with a generous portion of whipped cream, and brought them to the table.

"What's the occasion?" Trey asked as he cut a piece with the side of his fork.

"It's *I have the best husband day*," she said.

"Is that a monthly holiday?" He put the piece of pie in his mouth and chewed slowly.

She laughed. "We can make it monthly, weekly or daily, if you wish, because you're always the best."

"As are you," he said, forking another piece of pie.

After dinner, Patricia researched Pete Dorsey while Trey worked on legal matters. She found a newspaper article about the terrible automobile accident that killed him, a head-on collision with a semi, and his obituary. For the second time, she said a prayer for his family, then she made copies of each document for her case file.

If Dorsey was murdered, the driver of the semi might have some connection to Dr. Gryoti. Or the driver might have received a payment from Gryoti or one of his companies. She checked the police report and jotted down the driver's name, address, and phone number.

Patricia's eyes stung from the lateness of the hour and all the research. It was too late tonight to start looking for a payoff, but she'd get on it tomorrow.

CHAPTER 8

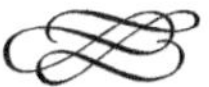

Patricia barely slept, her thoughts consumed by Ellery's warning of the dangers of investigating Gryoti.

She got up with Trey and went into the bathroom to prepare for the day. The faint creak of the old floorboards beneath her feet echoed through the otherwise silent house, a reminder of the home's storied past.

Over breakfast with Trey, she forced herself to smile, but her mind continued to churn with unanswered questions and festering doubts. Every bite of food felt mechanical, her focus elsewhere.

After Trey left for work, Patricia slipped into her running shoes and stepped onto the treadmill tucked in the corner of what had once been a Victorian sitting room, its ornate crown molding and faded wallpaper contrasting sharply with the modern equipment. The rhythmic pounding of her feet did little to ease her tension. Instead, her mind raced faster than her steps. Uncovering knowledgeable whistle-blowers could put her directly in Gryoti's crosshairs, But it was a risk she had to take for Isabel and Lucius.

While she showered, a fog of steam curled around the antique brass fixtures and clawfoot tub that hinted at the house's late-19th century origins. Where could she find whistleblowers? Certainly those who left scathing reviews of Magnum Oncology could be potential sources. And there were witnesses from previous cases against Magnum and Gryoti if she could unearth their names.

Names. She needed names. Lots of them. But even then, finding someone brave enough to speak out seemed almost impossible. Ellery had warned her: Gryoti was not the type of man anyone crossed lightly. Her stomach churned at the thought. She couldn't shake the image of Dorsey's lifeless body—a stark reminder of what might await anyone who dared expose the truth about Gryoti's operation.

After dressing for the day, she went to the office at the front of the house, opened her laptop, and pulled up her case file. She jotted down the few names she already had, but she needed more. Trey could help; he might be able to get access to the records from cases against Gryoti. But she'd have to approach him carefully. He needed to understand just how high the stakes were without feeling she was dragging him into danger.

Once Patricia had looked up phone numbers and addresses for the names she'd listed, she hesitated, her fingers tracing the intricate wood grain of the massive oak desk that had been in Trey's family for decades. Cold-calling strangers who might hold the key to unraveling Gryoti's empire felt daunting. She needed help. She picked up her phone and called Meredith.

"What can I do for you, sugar?" Meredith's familiar voice brought a small measure of relief.

"Like I mentioned last night, I'm investigating Magnum Oncology. I'm just getting started, so I'm trying to build a list of folks to interview who might have some dirt on Magnum's activities," Patricia explained.

"Potential whistleblowers."

"Exactly. Would you mind coming over and helping me develop more leads?"

"Now?"

"Are you available?"

"Yes. I'll be right over."

A HALF HOUR LATER, PATRICIA AND MEREDITH SAT AT Patricia's kitchen table, the warm light from a wrought-iron chandelier illuminating the worn, wide-plank floors beneath them and the slightly uneven plaster walls that whispered of centuries past. Every so often, Patricia glanced at the back window, half expecting to see someone watching.

"So, we need to find folks who have an axe to grind with Gryoti," Meredith said, focusing on the blank pad in front of her. "People who are really angry with him. Not just patients."

"He has an adult daughter, but he attended the gala with a girlfriend," Patricia said. "If he's divorced, it might be worth talking to his ex-wife. Nothing like a woman scorned as a source of unfavorable information on a man."

"Good idea," Meredith said. "And as a businessman, he's probably had plenty of major financial transactions. I'll check his credit report to see if there's any problems there. Blown off creditors certainly have an axe to grind."

"Back to the woman scorned thing," Patricia added, "he's probably got a string of ex-girlfriends. But how do we identify them?"

"The ex-wife might know some of them. And Savannah is a small town. I can check with some of the movers and shakers I know about Gryoti's dating habits."

"How do we find more dissatisfied patients?" Patricia asked, her voice tinged with desperation.

Meredith stared into space for a minute, her brow furrowed. Then she smiled. "Social media. There must be a local online cancer support group. Maybe more than one. Join the group, read the comments for mentions of Magnum. Also, ask the group: Can anyone share their experiences at Magnum Oncology? Just don't use your real name in case Gryoti monitors the site."

"That's a peach of an idea," Patricia said, her energy returning. "And I can raise the same question in the 'What's Happening in Savannah' Facebook group."

Meredith leaned back in her chair, her smile fading into a frown. "Be careful, Patricia. If Gryoti or his people catch wind of this, they won't just sit back and let you dig around."

Patricia nodded, her throat tightening. "I know the risks. But I can't stop now. I owe it to Isabel and Lucius."

"We make a good team," Meredith said, a hint of unease still lingering in her voice.

"Yes, we do. Thank you. Any more ideas?"

"Not right now." Meredith stood, her gaze lingering on Patricia. "I'll think more on the subject at the office and get back to you if I come up with anything else. Just promise me you'll be careful."

Patricia walked Meredith to the door where they embraced warmly. As the door clicked shut, Patricia leaned against it, her breath hitching. She couldn't fail, not with Lucius's life hanging in the balance.

DETERMINED TO TAKE THE NEXT STEP, PATRICIA RETURNED TO her desk and stared at the first name on her list: a woman who had left an unfavorable review about Magnum Oncology. She dialed the number with trembling fingers, half expecting it to no longer be in service. To her relief, a voice answered.

"Hello?"

"Hi, this is Patricia Falcon. I'm investigating some irregularities at Magnum Oncology, and your name came up as someone who might have insight. Can we talk?"

There was a long pause on the other end of the line. "I don't know how you got my name, but I don't want any trouble," the woman said, low and wary.

"I understand," Patricia said. "But you might have information that could help me stop something terrible. You'd be protected."

Another pause. "You don't know what you're getting into," the woman whispered, before abruptly hanging up.

Patricia stared at the phone, her heart racing. The fear in the woman's voice was unmistakable. She jotted a note to follow up later but knew that wasn't going to be easy.

As she turned toward her computer to research the next lead, a movement outside the front window caught her eye. A black sedan she hadn't noticed before idled across the street, its windows tinted too dark to see inside. Patricia's stomach tightened. She froze, watching, but after a few moments, the car pulled away, leaving her with more questions than answers.

Half an hour later, Patricia's phone buzzed, jolting her from her thoughts. Meredith's name flashed on the screen.

"Hey, Meredith," Patricia said.

"Good news. I have four more names for you, all ex-girlfriends of Gryoti. I'll text them right over to you."

"Thank you." Patricia smiled to herself. Meredith had a rare talent for getting important information. "Are they local?"

"Yes. My friend said each of them spent at least a year with Gryoti. Plus, I'm sending you the name of a local contractor who has a large judgement against Gryoti. Apparently, Gryoti doesn't pay if he's dissatisfied with the work."

"Much appreciation."

After hanging up, Patricia opened her laptop and navigated to a local cancer support group's forum. The posts were a mix of hope and heartbreak, but one thread stood out: complaints about billing and care at Magnum Oncology. One commenter, a user named Hope4Cure, had shared a detailed account of malpractice. Using an anonymous email account she'd set up for the investigation, Patricia drafted a private message, her fingers hovering over the keyboard before typing: *I'd like to hear more about your experience with Magnum. Can we talk?*

She hit send and exhaled, the weight of the day pressing on her shoulders. A new lead, but also new risks. Patricia's gaze drifted back to the window where the black sedan had been. Savannah's quiet, cobblestone streets suddenly felt far less safe.

Next up, Patricia contacted the clerk of the Chatham Superior Court and got the name of Gryoti's ex-wife. She'd retained his last name, and her phone number was listed. Patricia made an appointment to talk with Elena Gryoti.

She called more former patients with varying degrees of success. She was burning through names fast and needed to pull all this together better. She knew just who to talk with.

The late afternoon sun slanted through the bay window of Summer's sitting room, casting warm pools of light on the hardwood floors. Patricia sat on the edge of the couch, a tablet in her lap and a stack of printed notes on the coffee table before her. Across from her, Summer leaned back in her armchair, her skin radiant in the golden light. Her messy bun seemed to defy gravity, giving her an air of effortless charm. She held a steaming cup of jasmine tea, her eyes focused intently on Patricia.

"This is what I've gathered so far," Patricia began, scrolling through the notes on her tablet. "Gryoti keeps an iron grip on everything. And his patients..." She paused, shaking her head. "They're either too desperate or too intimidated to challenge anything he says."

Summer tilted her head, her expression thoughtful. "And what does that tell you about him?"

Patricia frowned. "That he's controlling, obviously. But it's more than that. He's built this whole image of himself as a miracle worker. Even when his treatments don't work, people still believe in him. It's almost... cult-like."

Summer nodded slowly, setting her teacup down on the table. "Cultlike is a good way to put it. People like Gryoti thrive on admiration and control. What you've told me reinforces my initial thought that he's showing strong narcissistic tendencies. He's created a world where he's the center of everything, and anyone who questions him is seen as a threat to that world."

"That makes sense," Patricia said. "But what about his staff? Why would they stay? Surely, they've seen the cracks in his facade."

"Fear, for one. But also, manipulation. Narcissists like him are masters at convincing people they're indispensable while simultaneously making them feel powerless. He's probably created an environment where his staff think they can't leave without risking everything—their jobs, their reputations, maybe even their safety."

Patricia's eyes narrowed. "So he's playing the savior and the tyrant at the same time."

"Exactly," Summer said. "And that's not all. You mentioned his patients. The way he preys on their desperation is classic sociopathic behavior. He's exploiting their vulnerability for his own gain, without a shred of empathy for the harm he's causing."

Patricia's grip tightened on the tablet. "I've seen some of the effects. Patients bankrupting themselves for treatments that don't work. Families torn apart by the stress. It's sickening."

Summer's voice softened, though her eyes remained sharp. "And that's his Achilles' heel, Patricia. People like him rely on fear and desperation to keep their power. But if you can shine a light on what he's doing, show people the truth, his house of cards will collapse."

Patricia nodded, determination hardening her features. "Then that's what I'll do. But I'll need your help. I need to understand him better in order to anticipate his moves."

Summer smiled faintly, her freckled face calm but resolute. "You've got it, darlin'. Keep breaking down his behavior, piece by piece, so we can figure out what makes him tick and where he's most vulnerable."

Patricia relaxed slightly, the weight on her shoulders feeling just a bit lighter. "Thank you, Summer. I don't know what I'd do without you."

Summer reached out, placing a gentle hand on Patricia's. "You're stronger than you think, Patricia. But I'm here for you, every step of the way."

The two women sat in the fading light, the quiet strength of their bond a steadfast anchor in the storm of their pursuit for justice.

CHAPTER 9

*T*rey appeared in the doorway of Patricia's office shortly after five. Her heart leapt at the sight of him, but the tension that had gripped her all day refused to let go. Outside, sunlight filtered through the Spanish moss that draped the live oaks lining their quiet Savannah street. She forced a smile and stood.

"You're home early," she said, smoothing the front of her blouse.

"Light workday," he replied, stepping into the room.

She crossed the space between them, and he gathered her into his arms. The faint scent of lemon from his aftershave filled her senses, grounding her in the moment. His embrace was strong yet gentle, and for a brief second, the stress of the day seemed to melt away.

"Are you okay?" Trey asked, pulling back slightly to study her face.

She nodded quickly. "Just a long day."

He brushed a strand of hair from her face, his touch warm and comforting. "Then let's make the evening better," he said in his warm, made-in-the-South voice.

Her voice softened. "I missed you."

"And I missed you," he replied, his deep-set brown eyes steady on hers. "You're the best part of my day, every day."

Her heart swelled, but the image of the black sedan parked outside their house earlier flickered across her mind. She leaned in, her kiss tender but lingering, as if trying to anchor herself in his presence.

"Are you hungry?" she asked when they finally stepped apart.

"Famished."

"I don't have anything planned. Do you want to go out?"

"Sure. Any suggestions?"

"Wherever you want," she replied.

He thought for a moment. "How about Vic's on the River?"

She smiled, the tension easing slightly. "Perfect. You and your Southern food."

"You're not complaining," he teased, glancing at his watch. "Six thirty?"

She nodded.

"I'll make the reservation," he said, pressing a kiss to her forehead before leaving.

Patricia wrapped up her casework on her laptop and moved to the window, her eyes scanning the street. The black sedan was gone, but the unease it had left behind clung to her. She turned away and headed upstairs to dress for dinner.

THEY ARRIVED AT VIC'S JUST BEFORE SIX THIRTY. THE HISTORIC cotton warehouse stood proud by the Savannah River, its weathered walls bathed in the warm glow of lanterns. The river shimmered in the twilight, its slow-moving waters reflecting the fading hues of the sunset.

Inside, they were promptly seated at a quiet corner table by the wine wall. Patricia glanced out the window. Across the street, partially hidden beneath the shadows of a live oak, was a dark sedan. Her chest tightened, and she quickly refocused on Trey as he reached for her hand.

"You're a million miles away," he said gently, his thumb tracing soft circles on her knuckles.

"Sorry," she murmured. "Just distracted."

The server arrived, her soft Southern drawl as warm as the golden light in the room. "Evening, y'all. Can I get you started with something to drink?"

They ordered a bottle of wine and their meals—crawfish beignets to start, and halibut glazed with bourbon for the main course.

As the wine was poured, Trey leaned in, his voice low and warm. "You said your day was long."

Patricia hesitated. Trust and honesty were the foundation of their relationship, but the truth felt heavy. She met his gaze and nodded. "And terrifying," she admitted.

His brow furrowed. "Why?"

"Gryoti is a bad person. He's not only a medical fraudster, but in all likelihood, a cold-blooded murderer."

Trey exhaled slowly. "How do you know that?"

"The last person to investigate him was killed in an auto accident. And today..." Her voice wavered, and she took a sip of wine to steady herself. "I think someone's been watching me."

His jaw tightened. "Watching you? What happened?"

"There was a black sedan parked outside the house this afternoon. I don't know if it's connected, but—"

"It's likely connected," Trey said firmly. "And you don't need this. Turn over what you have to the FBI and let them handle it."

"I can't, Trey. Lucius's life is at stake. For everything he and Isabel have done for us over the years, I owe him. I know investigations come with risks, but I won't let danger divert me. Ever. We live with danger. We prevail. And I intend to prevail here."

"Okay. Then let's get our defenses sharpened. I know my marksmanship is rusty. How about we go to the shooting range tomorrow morning."

"Don't you have work?"

"Nothing that important."

"Sure." She knew how perishable marksmanship expertise was, and she'd been neglecting target practice lately.

"How much do you know about Gryoti's pattern of life?" he asked.

"I haven't started on that yet. I prioritized finding whistleblowers."

"That's reasonable. But if he's as dangerous as you think he is, we want to know him well enough to anticipate his every move. Do you want me to put Simon on it? It's a time-consuming task, and it appears you could use the help while you continue searching for whistleblowers."

"Good idea, Trey. I'll contact Simon when we get home."

He nodded. "Is there anything else I can help with?"

She pulled a folded list from her purse and handed it to him. "These are past cases against Gryoti. I'd like to talk to the plaintiffs, see what evidence they had. I think I'll have more success if the initial contact comes from a fellow attorney. But I hate to involve—"

"It's no problem," Trey interrupted, tucking the list into his jacket pocket. "You said it yourself. We've always lived with danger."

Her eyes softened. "Are you sure?"

"Always," he said, his voice steady.

As they left Vic's, the gas lanterns lining the cobblestone

streets flickered softly, their light reflected in the puddles left by an afternoon rain.

Patricia's gaze drifted to the dark sedan still parked under the shadow of a nearby oak. Her pulse quickened, but Trey's hand on the small of her back grounded her.

"We're fine," he murmured.

In the Bentley, Patricia couldn't shake the feeling they were being followed. The headlights in the rearview mirror seemed too persistent, too deliberate.

"Trey," she said quietly.

"I see it," he replied, his tone calm but alert.

He turned onto a side street, then another, weaving through Savannah's maze of squares. The headlights continued straight, and Patricia exhaled, her shoulders slumping.

"Probably nothing," Trey said, squeezing her hand.

"Probably," she echoed, though the knot in her stomach remained.

When they reached home, Trey wrapped an arm around her waist as they walked inside.

"No matter what happens, we've got this," he said, his lips brushing against her hair.

Patricia leaned into him, drawing strength from his presence. But as the door closed behind them, her thoughts lingered on the shadows outside.

Later that evening, Patricia sat at her desk, staring at the monitor displaying their home security camera footage. Trey had gone upstairs to shower, leaving her alone with her thoughts and the unnerving footage she was now replaying for the third time.

The black sedan appeared on the screen again, time-stamped 3:07 p.m. It idled across the street for nearly five minutes before slowly driving away. Patricia leaned closer, her eyes narrowing. The angle made it impossible to see the driver clearly, but there was a good enough angle on the windshield to definitely see someone in the car. She paused the video, scrutinizing the grainy outline of the figure. A chill ran through her as questions swirled in her mind.

Was this just paranoia, or was someone really watching her?

A faint creak from the hallway startled her. She spun around to see Trey leaning against the doorframe dressed in navy pajamas, his hair still damp.

"You're obsessing," he said gently, stepping into the room.

She sighed and rubbed her temples. "I don't think it's nothing, Trey.

Trey walked over and placed his hands on her shoulders, his touch firm yet reassuring. "We'll figure it out. But you need to rest. This isn't going to solve itself tonight."

As he spoke, the doorbell rang. Patricia stiffened, her heart pounding.

"You heard that, right?" she whispered.

Trey nodded, his expression darkening. He moved toward the front door, grabbing the loaded shotgun they kept in the foyer table.

"Stay here," he said firmly.

Patricia followed a step behind, unwilling to let him face whatever was out there alone. After checking the live video feed, Trey opened the door cautiously. The porch was empty, the night eerily still. A faint breeze rustled the oaks lining the street.

Then Patricia saw it—a folded piece of paper lying on the welcome mat.

Trey bent down to pick it up, his grip tightening on the

shotgun. He unfolded the note, scanned the words, and showed it to Patricia.

Stop digging, or you'll regret it.

Patricia's stomach dropped. Her fingers trembled as she took the note from Trey. The handwriting was jagged, almost frantic.

Trey closed the door and locked it, turning to her with a grim expression. "This just became personal."

Patricia swallowed hard, the weight of the message pressing down on her. "It already was."

As they sat on the couch, Trey's arm around her shoulders, Patricia couldn't shake the image of the car or the threatening words from the note.

"How did Gryoti find out you were investigating him?" Trey asked.

"I've been talking with people," she said. "Maybe someone got back to him. Oh my gosh," she said. "This is evidence." She bolted up, went to her office, grabbed an envelope, dropped the note into it, and logged the date, time, and place they found the note on the envelope. Then she sealed it, put it into a folder labeled evidence, and returned to the family room.

"We should check the security video," she said.

"Already have." Trey held up his phone. "A drone delivered the note and pressed the doorbell."

"And whoever was manipulating the drone was well beyond our cameras?"

"Yes," Trey said, his voice steady but concerned. "I think we should call Simon. I know you don't want a bodyguard, but this isn't just a random threat."

She shook her head. "Not yet. If I bring in security, I'll lose what little advantage I have. Whoever dropped that note will know I'm scared, and I can't afford to show weakness."

Trey's jaw tightened, but he didn't argue. Instead, he

pulled her closer, his voice softening. "I'm here. Whatever happens, we face it together."

Patricia leaned into him, closing her eyes as his warmth and steady presence anchored her. But deep down, she knew the game had changed. Gryoti—or whoever was behind this—wasn't just playing intimidation games anymore.

Somewhere outside, the shadows held secrets, and Patricia would have to uncover them before they consumed her.

CHAPTER 10

Patricia woke later than usual, savoring the rare luxury of a slow morning with Trey. They shared a leisurely breakfast at Goose Feathers Café, the air filled with the inviting aroma of coffee and warm pastries. The cheerful hum of conversations mixed with the clink of silverware against plates, but Patricia's thoughts were elsewhere. The cryptic note on their doorstep weighed on her, as did the unsettling presence of the black sedan that seemed to haunt her every move.

After breakfast, they made their way to the Quickshot Shooting Range in Trey's Bentley, its smooth ride doing little to soothe her nerves. Patricia sat quietly, her Kimber nestled in her purse, its familiar weight both reassuring and insufficient. As they pulled into the range's parking lot, she unlocked the slide of her pistol and cleared the chamber, her movements deliberate. The empty firearm left her feeling exposed, a vulnerability that gnawed at her.

The range greeted them with the faint tang of gun oil in the air and the muted pop of gunfire in the distance. Patricia followed Trey through the lobby, where they signed in and collected their gear.

Once inside, the firing line buzzed with controlled chaos: muffled voices, the sharp staccato of gunshots, and the rhythmic beeping of electronic target systems. Patricia donned her protective eyewear and earmuffs, their snug fit insulating her from the noise. She approached her assigned stall, the steel partitions cold and unyielding under her touch.

Setting her first target at five yards was meditative. A small ritual of control in an unpredictable world. Patricia inserted a loaded magazine, chambered a round, and steadied her two-hand grip. She raised the Kimber, aligning the sights with practiced precision. At a natural respiratory pause, she eased the trigger back. The first shot cracked through the air, the recoil of her 45 jolting her arms. The muzzle flashed briefly, and the target shuddered as a neat hole appeared dead center. She fired twice more in measured succession, forming a tight triangle on the paper.

Satisfied, she adjusted her grip, switching the Kimber to her strong hand. Each movement was deliberate, honed through years of practice. The shots rang out again, their sharp retorts punctuating the quiet intensity of her focus. She reloaded, this time firing with her weak hand. The grouping spread slightly, as she expected, but every shot hit the target.

She exhaled slowly, lowering the Kimber and letting her arms relax. The rhythm of the shooting was calming, a stark contrast to the turmoil brewing in her mind. She wasn't just practicing. She was preparing.

This was more than practice. It was affirmation. In her life, danger wasn't theoretical; it was woven into her history. Over the past decade, she had witnessed humanity at its worst—murderers, kidnappers, predators. Criminals who thrived on fear and intimidation. She carried scars, both seen and unseen, from being hunted by people like Gryoti. But she'd always fought back-fiercely, decisively. Gryoti was no different. The thought of his attempted intimidation sent a surge of determination through her. The Kimber wasn't just a tool; it was a statement. She carried it to say, "You won't take my life from me."

She adjusted the target to ten yards and repeated the sequence, her grip steady and sure. The grouping held tight. Her precision was not born from an abstract desire for power but a hard-earned understanding: the world didn't allow room for naivety. Protecting herself, her family, and her community wasn't a choice; it was a responsibility.

Each squeeze of the trigger was a reminder of why she prepared like this. There was no room for complacency when the stakes were life and death. Occasionally, she became the hunter herself, tracking those who preyed on the innocent. In those moments, when the line between survival and justice blurred, she couldn't afford to falter. Every shot, every movement, had to be perfect. Justice depended on it. Her survival demanded it.

Patricia glanced briefly at Trey, who was focused on his own target, his movements smooth and confident. A moment of gratitude passed over her. He understood her need to prepare, to protect herself, even if he didn't fully grasp the weight of her fears.

At fifteen yards, the challenge grew. Her two-hand shots were less precise, the groupings wider, but still within the target's center mass. Patricia inhaled deeply, focusing on the rhythm of her breathing as she reloaded. There was peace in this ritual. Each repetition tightened her focus, steeled her nerves. She knew what it meant to face danger head-on. She knew the terrible weight of hesitating when it mattered most.

For Patricia, carrying a gun wasn't about fear. It was about readiness, about owning the role her marriage had thrust upon her. There were wolves in the world, and sometimes, she had to be the one to stop them.

She fired again at fifteen yards, the shots ringing out with steady precision. This time, the groupings were tighter.

She let out a long breath as the last round fired, the echo fading into the hum of the range. Patricia unloaded the Kimber, locking the slide back, and stepped from the stall. Her hands were steady. Her heart was calm.

This wasn't just practice. This was survival. Justice. She had faced danger before, and she would face it again. And when the time came, she would be ready.

PATRICIA'S HEART RACED AS SIMON'S SLEEK, BLACK SUV parked at the front of the house. Midday sun glinted off its polished exterior, momentarily blinding her. She glanced at her watch—12:57 p.m. Right on time.

Simon, her occasional bodyguard and technical guru, stepped out, his tall frame silhouetted against the bright autumn light. His movements were sharp and purposeful, his dark tactical shirt stretched taut across his broad shoulders as he slung a black backpack over one arm. At the door, she greeted him with a quick hug, her hands brushing against the rough fabric of his shirt.

"Thanks for coming over," she said.

A faint smile curved his lips, but his brown eyes flickered past her, scanning her foyer. "Always happy to help," he said.

She stepped aside, letting him in. The house felt suddenly too quiet, the ticking of the grandfather clock amplified in the stillness.

He was a commanding presence—tall, broad-shouldered, and dressed in his usual all-black ensemble. His form-fitting

T-shirt highlighted the powerful build beneath, and his cargo pants and scuffed boots bore the marks of countless missions. But it was his face that drew her attention, as it always did. Rugged and scarred, with soulful caramel eyes that seemed to see everything.

At the dining table, Simon set his backpack down with a soft thud and unzipped it, each motion deliberate and calculated. He pulled out a black laptop, his fingers moving with precision as he powered it on.

"So," he began, his eyes fixed on the loading screen, "you've started a new investigation."

"I have. Do you need anything? Coffee? Iced tea? Water?"

He glanced at her, his calm demeanor radiating an unshakable confidence. "I'm fine, thanks."

She gestured to the chair across from her. "Sit. Let's get started."

Simon sat, his movements fluid, like a predator settling in before the hunt.

"I'm investigating possible medical fraud," she said as she sat. "The alleged perpetrator is Dr. Dimitri Gryoti, a well-known local oncologist. I need a pattern-of-life profile on him." She slid a beige folder across the table, the edges of the papers inside slightly dog-eared. "This is everything I know so far."

Simon opened the folder and thumbed through it, his eyes darting over each page with the intensity of someone solving a puzzle. "Not bad," he said finally, though his tone was devoid of emotion.

"Thanks, but it's hardly complete." She leaned forward, her hands clasped tightly in her lap. "Do you have time to build one for me?"

He paused, brushing back a strand of dark hair that had fallen into his face. His brow furrowed. "When do you need it?"

"As soon as possible. But be careful," she added quickly, her fingers fidgeting with the edge of her sleeve. "I'm only a couple of days in, and I've already gotten a warning note."

Simon's hand froze for the briefest moment before he resumed flipping through the folder. His gaze flicked up to meet hers, dark brown and unflinching. "Understood."

Patricia's throat tightened. "This guy's dangerous, Simon. He's killed at least one investigator, and his fraud has indirectly killed patients by denying them proper care."

Simon's jaw tightened. "We'll take him down," he said.

"Anything else you need from me?"

He shook his head. "Do you mind if I start now?"

"Not at all. What's the plan?"

"First, I'll set up surveillance tools. We'll let them run for a few days to establish his routines. Then we'll track deviations and adjust accordingly."

"Will you also create a relationship map on him?"

"Sure. I can do that."

"Sounds good." Patricia pushed back her chair, the wooden legs scraping softly against the floor. "I'll be in the front office if you need me. There's a fresh pot of Black Rifle coffee on the burner."

"Got it."

The hallway to her office felt longer than usual, the faint creak of the floorboards under her heels echoing in the quiet house. Her phone buzzed in her pocket, making her jump. She swiped to answer. "Meredith?"

Meredith's voice came quick and clipped, the sound of typing in the background. "I've started forensic accounting on Gryoti's bank and credit card records. Not much domestically on his business, just supplier payments and patient transfers. The surplus from the business funds his extravagant lifestyle, and even then, a hefty amount goes overseas.

I'm also using blockchain tools to trace his crypto transactions. He's hiding profits."

Patricia pressed a hand to her forehead. "Good work. Keep Simon in the loop—he's doing a pattern-of-life profile."

"Will do."

By the time Patricia returned to Simon, the air in the house felt thicker, like it was holding its breath. She paused in the doorway, watching him work. His eyes were locked on the laptop screen, his fingers flying across the keyboard with practiced ease.

"Coffee?" she asked.

"Please," he said without looking up.

She poured two cups, the rich aroma of the brew cutting through the tension in the room. She handed him a mug and sat in the chair beside him.

"How's it going?"

"Good," he said, his tone clipped and efficient. "I've begun the relationship map. The web crawler's gathering data on him. I've tapped his cellphone and placed WireShark in Magnum's network to monitor their communications. Meredith sent over his credit card numbers, so I'm now monitoring his charges. GPS tracking is next—car and smartwatch. Once that's up, we'll analyze his travel patterns. Now we wait."

"Impressive." She took a sip of her coffee; the warmth settled her nerves slightly. But she couldn't shake the feeling that with Gryoti on the prowl waiting was the most dangerous part.

The clinic was quiet. After hours. He preferred it that way.

Gryoti walked the dim hallways like a general inspecting his fortress. The scent of bleach hung heavy—sterility and secrecy in equal measure. He paused before entering his office, letting his hand rest on the biometric scanner. The door unlocked with a sigh.

Inside, the office radiated credibility: sleek white cabinetry, frosted glass partitions, chrome-accented lighting. His vanity wall greeted him like a shrine—photos with senators, celebrities, medical luminaries. Smiling handshakes frozen in time. Impressions mattered. They always had.

Carol followed him in, holding her tablet like a weapon.

"It's confirmed," she said without preamble. "Your network was probed. The IP is tied Simon Stone. Works with Falcon."

Gryoti moved to his desk, tapped the surface to light the screen.

"They accessed the sandbox?" he asked.

"Yes, but only partially. Our obfuscation worked. Still, he's good."

Gryoti steepled his fingers. The edges of his watch glinted in the low light. "They're close. Too close."

Carol shifted. "Shall I initiate firewall layering and diversion protocols?"

"Not just that. I want a full decoy environment—make it convincing. Give them false treatment protocols. Patient testimonials. Let them waste their time chasing smoke."

He stood and walked to the bin in the corner. Its lid was sealed. Inside were the remnants of the day's infusions, each container traceable, damning. Each to be burned by him personally. He ran his hand along the metal. Cold. Necessary.

"Patricia Falcon lit a fire," he said, his voice silk over steel. "And I intend to make sure it burns her house down before mine."

CHAPTER 12

*A*fter Simon left, Patricia paced her office, muted light from the Tiffany desk lamp casting long shadows across the room.

Then she sat and opened her incoming email. One message, from Clinic, caught her attention. She opened it.

You don't follow advice well. Stop your investigation now, or we'll send you back to the flames of hell.

Patricia touched the scars on her arm as she vividly remembered the Paris fireball that sent her to the hospital, and the subsequent events that nearly cost her life. How did Gryoti know about that? How did he know she still feared open flames?

The air felt heavy with frustration, but she forced herself to focus. To move forward. Picking up her phone, she dialed Willie, one of the few media people she could trust.

"Hello, Patricia," Willie answered, his voice steady and familiar. "How's your investigation going?"

"It's off to a rocky start," Patricia admitted, the strain in her voice unmistakable. "The first person I approached shut me down completely. She was my best lead, Willie. I thought she'd cooperate, but she didn't even give me a chance."

"That's tough," Willie said, his tone sympathetic. "But building trust takes time, you know that. You can't just barge in expecting answers."

"I know." Patricia sighed, running a hand through her hair. "I screwed up. Burned a resource I couldn't afford to lose."

"You'll figure it out," Willie said. "You always do."

Patricia leaned against the edge of the oak desk, the round corner pressing into her hip. "Thanks for the vote of confidence. By the way, when was the last time you talked to Dr. Gryoti?"

"Gryoti?" Willie hesitated. "That was... five years ago, I think. Why?"

"I need him to slip up," Patricia said, her voice hardening. "What do you think about interviewing him for a feature article? Make it about his highly successful practice, but push him enough to get him making false claims about his treatments."

Willie let out a low chuckle. "Patricia, you're as cunning as ever. Risky, but it could work. I'll look into it."

"Let me know what you find," she urged. "Even the smallest detail could help."

"You've got it. If he talks, I'll send you the full recording."

As Patricia ended the call, a surge of determination coursed through her veins. Because of Lucius's health, time was slipping away, and the pressure to quickly find answers felt like a noose tightening around her neck.

She dialed Beau Simpson, her first ally in this labyrinthine investigation.

"Hello, Patricia. What's up?" Beau greeted, his voice casual but tinged with curiosity.

"I need your help, again," Patricia said, skipping any

pleasantries. "First, thanks for recommending Ellery Hampton. She was a lifesaver."

"She's great, isn't she?" Beau replied warmly. "What's going on now?"

"I've uncovered three drugs linked to Gryoti's patients: Blanscan, Stemase, and Dustare. Do those names ring any bells?"

A heavy silence filled the line. Patricia could almost hear Beau's mind working, sifting through his knowledge.

"Blanscan is a fake drug," Beau said finally. "The FDA flagged it years ago. The other two? I've never heard of them. Ghost drugs, maybe. If you can prove Gryoti's prescribing Blanscan, he's guilty of malpractice—or worse."

"That's exactly what I needed to hear," Patricia said, relief flooding her voice.

"I'll dig into it," Beau offered. "I know some local oncologists who might have heard rumors about Gryoti. I'll see what they have to say."

"Be careful, Beau," Patricia warned, gripping the phone tighter. "He's dangerous. I've already received a warning note, and I'm taking it seriously."

"A warning note?" Beau's voice sharpened. "What makes you think it's more than just bluster?"

"Pete Dorsey," Patricia said, her words weighted with meaning. "He was investigating Gryoti for the FBI when he died in a car accident. I don't think it was a coincidence."

Beau exhaled sharply. "Okay, I'll tread carefully."

When Patricia ended the call, unease settled over her like a dark cloud. She called to see if Summer was available to help her sort through the new developments.

PATRICIA SAT ACROSS FROM SUMMER AT THE SMALL, ROUND table in Summer's kitchen. The warm aroma of freshly brewed coffee mingled with the soft hum of a ceiling fan overhead. Summer's eyes were intent, her fine-boned hands wrapped around a delicate porcelain cup. She leaned forward slightly, her messy auburn bun bobbing with the movement.

"I'm hitting walls with these whistleblowers," Patricia admitted, frustration tinging her voice. "Most of them are too scared to talk, and the ones who do want to talk say they're bound by NDAs. It's like they've given up hope."

Summer nodded slowly, her face thoughtful. "It's not uncommon for people to feel trapped in situations like this. Fear—whether it's fear of losing their livelihood, facing retaliation, or simply being ostracized—can be paralyzing. But there are ways to help them see beyond that fear."

"How?" Patricia asked, leaning in. "How do I convince them that speaking out is worth the risk?"

Summer set her cup down gently, her fingers interlacing as she rested her hands on the table. "Empathy is your most powerful tool here, Patricia. People who feel heard and understood are more likely to open up. Start by showing them you're not just interested in their information, but in their well-being. Ask about their fears, their concerns, and what's keeping them from speaking out."

Patricia nodded, jotting notes in her notebook. "I can do that. But what about the NDAs? Some of them seem convinced they'll be sued into oblivion if they say anything."

"Reframe the situation for them," Summer advised. "Help them see their disclosures not as breaking an agreement, but as fulfilling a higher duty. Remind them that by staying silent, they're allowing Gryoti to continue preying on others. Frame their choice as a moral one—a chance to protect future victims and possibly save lives."

"So, appeal to their sense of justice," Patricia said, scribbling more notes.

"Exactly. But you need to balance that with reassurance. Make it clear they won't be alone in this. Offer them support and resources. Let them know you'll do everything in your power to protect their identity and ensure they're not left to fend for themselves."

Patricia looked up, her expression softening. "You make it sound so straightforward."

Summer smiled, her face kind but resolute. "It's not, darlin'. It takes patience, trust, and sometimes a little bit of luck. But if you approach them with genuine care and integrity, most people will respond. They just need to believe that doing the right thing is not only possible but also necessary."

Patricia exhaled slowly, a small smile tugging at the corners of her mouth. "I'm so glad I came to you with this, Summer. You always know how to cut through the noise."

Summer reached across the table and gave Patricia's hand a gentle squeeze. "You've got this, Patricia. Just keep your heart open and your mind sharp. These people need you to be their anchor. And I'm always here if you need me."

Patricia squeezed back, the weight on her shoulders feeling just a little lighter. "Thank you, Summer. I'll let you know how it goes."

As Patricia gathered her notes and prepared to leave, she felt a renewed sense of purpose. The path ahead might still be fraught with challenges, but with Summer's guidance, she was more confident than ever in her ability to navigate it.

Once home, Patricia went to the kitchen, her mind whirring as she mechanically prepped shrimp and grits. The comforting aroma of butter and garlic filled the air, but it did little to soothe her nerves.

While taking out the trash, an idea struck her like a bolt of lightning. She froze on the driveway, her heart racing. Magnum's garbage—could it hold the evidence she needed?

She darted back inside and called Simon.

"Simon, are you up for a dumpster dive tonight?"

"Always," Simon replied without hesitation. "What time?"

"Midnight," Patricia said. "Come by at eleven thirty so we can plan."

"Done," Simon said, the line clicking off.

Patricia returned to the kitchen, forcing herself to focus on finishing dinner. "Dinner in five," she called to Trey, who was reading in the family room.

Over plates of steaming shrimp and creamy grits, she explained her plan.

"A dumpster dive?" Trey said, raising an eyebrow. "That's bold, even for you."

"I don't have a choice," Patricia said firmly. "If I can find used containers of those fake drugs, it could crack this case wide open."

Trey nodded. "Good plan, but you'll need more hands. Bring in your whole team. It'll go faster."

"You're right," Patricia said, already mentally forming her call list.

By eleven thirty, Simon arrived with Meredith, Summer, and Timnit Araya, a retired Ranger who often assisted Patricia with her investigations. The night air was thick and cool, the garage lights casting a harsh glow over the assembled group.

"Here's the plan," Patricia said, her voice brisk. "Simon will grab the trash from Magnum. We'll sort through it here, looking for anything tied to *Blanscan*, *Stemase*, or *Dustare*."

"What about protective gear?" Meredith asked, crossing her arms.

"We improvise," Patricia said. "Safety glasses from target practice, gloves Simon brought, and garbage bags for gowns."

It wasn't ideal, but it would have to do.

Not long after midnight, Simon returned to Patricia's

garage with a dozen overstuffed trash bags, their contents reeking of chemicals and decay.

"Let's get to work," Patricia said, snapping on her gloves.

The team worked in tense silence, the only sounds the rustling of plastic and the occasional groan of disgust. The stench was suffocating, and the task painstaking.

"Nothing," Meredith muttered, tossing an empty wrapper into a bin.

"Lots of used medical supplies," Summer added, her gloved hands trembling slightly, "but nothing tied to the drugs."

After an hour, they were finished. Patricia leaned against the picnic table they'd set up, her eyes scanning the trash-strewn garage.

"We found nothing. Where did Magnum's infusion supplies go?" she said aloud, frustration evident in her tone. "Is someone erasing the evidence?"

"Probably," Timnit said. "If they're careful enough, they wouldn't leave anything behind."

Patricia nodded grimly. "It's a dead end, but not *the* end. We'll find another way."

They stripped off their makeshift gear, cleaned up, and headed inside. Patricia poured wine for everyone, the crimson liquid shimmering under the kitchen lights.

"Not the outcome I hoped for," she admitted, "but thank you all."

Simon raised his glass. "We'll get them next time."

The others nodded, clinking their glasses as resolve hardened in their expressions.

CHAPTER 13

$\mathcal{B}$y the time Patricia awoke the following morning, light spilled through the bedroom sheers in muted streaks, fractured by the skeletal branches outside. The faint hum of birdsong was subdued, almost hesitant, blending with the whisper of wind. Trey had already left for work, leaving behind the trace of his lemon aftershave, a scent that now seemed too sharp, too fleeting. Despite the lingering memory of last night's dumpster dive failure, Patricia had slept deeply, her exhaustion overpowering the sense of unease she always felt during investigations. This morning, though, tension clung to her, subtle but insistent, like the edge of an approaching storm just out of sight.

After slipping into her workout clothes, Patricia spent an hour on the treadmill. The steady rhythm of her steps and the driving beat of her playlist failed to calm the restless energy coursing through her. Her body burned with effort, but her thoughts wandered back to Gryoti, his unnervingly composed smile. Post workout, the hot shower offered some reprieve, but it wasn't enough to wash away the unease threading through her. She dressed in a cashmere sweater and slim jeans, her mind already leaping ahead to the tasks of the day.

Downstairs, the kitchen greeted her with its usual warmth, but even the familiar ritual of feeding the feral cats felt oddly disconnected. The cats, sleek and confident, darted cautious glances over their shoulders as they ate, their ears twitching at sounds Patricia couldn't hear. She closed the back door, split a bagel, and popped it into the toaster.

As she waited, she poured herself a mug of coffee, the dark, rich aroma offering fleeting comfort. She stood at the window, staring out at the backyard. Usually a sanctuary, the scene felt different today—foreboding somehow. The towering split-leaf philodendron swayed in the wind like a sentinel keeping watch. The China palms loomed tall, their shadows flickering against the fence. Spanish moss hung from the oak tree, its movement too slow, too deliberate in the breeze.

The sharp pop of the toaster made her jump, the sound snapping her back to the present. She retrieved the bagel, her movements brisk as she spread cream cheese over each half. Sitting at the table, she sipped her coffee, its bitterness grounding her. The taste reminded her of Trey, of their mornings together. His absence and the silence of the house pressed against her, heavier than usual.

Patricia glanced at her phone, opening her to-do list. The first task: send the gala photos to Timnit. She tapped through her gallery, pausing on each image. The faces were sharp, the expressions telling—some curious, some tense. Gryoti stood at the center of it all, his demeanor calm, but his eyes shadowed with something Patricia couldn't quite place. She sent the photos to Timnit, then punched in Timnit's number.

"Hello, Patricia. How are you doing?" Timnit's voice was steady, but Patricia thought she detected a hint of weariness beneath the calm.

"Fine, thanks. Sorry about the garbage mess last night. How are you?"

"I'm good. Just wading through emails. I assume you want facial recognition on everyone in the photos?"

"Yes. Simon is building a relationship map on Gryoti. I'd bet the people Gryoti's talking to in those photos are worth mapping."

"Understood. Any rush on this?"

"Not really."

"Well, I have a quiet day ahead. I'll prioritize it and should have results quickly, maybe an hour."

Patricia hesitated. Timnit rarely sounded vulnerable, but today there was something raw in her tone. Her husband's latest deployment had stretched on far too long.

"Do you want to come over for coffee after you're done?" Patricia offered, keeping her voice light.

"Sure," Timnit replied after a pause, the slight softening in her tone unmistakable.

Shortly after hanging up, the doorbell rang. After checking the security camera, Patricia opened it to find Sheila holding a bouquet of fall-colored mums. Her gray hair was pulled back into a ponytail, and she wore pink overalls with her florist logo on the left pocket. Her smile seemed to fill her wrinkle-free face. Age had been kind to her.

"They're beautiful," Patricia said as she watched Sheila remove the old flowers from the foyer table and replace them with the new ones.

"Glad you like them. They just arrived fresh this morning."

"Lots of deliveries today?"

Sheila nodded, smiling.

"Have you ever heard of Dr. Gryoti?"

"The guy on TV?"

"Yes. Has he or Magnum Oncology ever bought flowers

from you?" Patricia asked, the casual lilt of her voice disguising her sharp intent.

Sheila's brows knit together. "No. Why do you ask?"

"I'm investigating him."

Sheila's ash-gray eyes widened, her hand pausing mid-air. "Really? I have a friend, Celeste Wright, who used to work at Magnum. She told me she left because of some shady practices there."

Patricia's pulse quickened, the hairs on her arms standing on end. "Do you suppose she'd be willing to talk to me about it? Off the record, of course."

"She's been pretty open with me. I'll ask her and let you know."

"Thanks, Sheila. I'd really appreciate it."

After Sheila left, Patricia returned to her office. As she sat at her desk, she stared out the window, watching Sheila's van disappear down the street. A flicker of movement in her peripheral vision drew her attention—a shadow slipping behind the oak tree at the edge of her yard. Her muscles tensed, but when she looked again, the space was empty. Perhaps an animal. She booted up her laptop and went to work.

A half hour later, her phone buzzed, breaking her focus. It was Timnit.

"Hey, is that coffee offer still good?"

"Always," Patricia said, already moving to the kitchen.

Ten minutes later, Timnit arrived. The two women hugged briefly before retreating to the kitchen.

"It's getting cooler out there," Timnit said.

Patricia nodded, her gaze steady but wary. "Let's get straight to it. What did you find?"

Timnit handed her a detailed report. "The current girl-friend is Carol Alberta, Gryoti's office manager. She's been there for three years. Several of the others in the photos are local healthcare officials. Two are prominent politicians, both recipients of Gryoti's donations."

Patricia scanned the document, her mind racing with questions. Some of the pieces were falling into place, but the gaps in the picture were troubling. "Impressive as always. Thank you, Timnit." Patricia leaned forward, her expression soft and empathetic. "When does David get back?"

Timnit's brown eyes glistened with unshed tears. "He gets back in the States next week and comes home the following week." Her voice trembled as she added, "I sure do miss him."

Patricia reached across the table and took Timnit's hand in both of hers. "Oh, Timnit, we all miss him. And we're so grateful for the work he's doing. But I know that doesn't make the waiting any easier for you." Her voice was tender, as though she could carry some of Timnit's pain in her words.

Timnit blinked rapidly, trying to keep the tears at bay. "It's been so long, you know? Five months of empty nights and wondering if he's okay. Not being able to tell him about all the little things. It's like… like half of me is missing."

Patricia's chest tightened. She squeezed Timnit's hand gently. "You're so strong. I don't know how you do it; you amaze me. And when David comes home, it'll be like the world's brightest light just switched back on. You deserve that happiness."

Timnit sat in silence for a moment, her loneliness etched into every line of her face. Then, with a small, shaky smile, she said, "We're going to a resort ranch in North Dakota after he gets back. Just the two of us. No cellphones. No internet. Totally off the grid."

Patricia's face lit up. "That sounds perfect. Peace, quiet, and time to reconnect. Have you planned any surprises for him?"

Timnit's smile grew more certain. "I'm putting together a

scrapbook of all the things he missed. Photos, little notes. I want him to feel like he was here, even though he wasn't."

Patricia's eyes shimmered with admiration. "That's beautiful, Timnit. He's going to love it. And it'll remind him how lucky he is to have you."

Timnit sighed deeply, her broad shoulders loosening as if a heavy weight had been lifted. "You always know the right thing to say, Patricia. Thank you."

Patricia gave her friend's hand one last reassuring squeeze. "That's what friends are for. And until David's back, I'm here for you—day or night, okay? You're not alone in this."

For the next hour, their conversation ebbed and flowed, touching on memories, dreams, and the little moments that kept Timnit going. Patricia laughed, listened, and shared stories that brought a flicker of joy back to Timnit's eyes.

When Timnit glanced at her watch, she sighed. "I'd better get going. Thanks for this, Patricia. Really."

Patricia stood and enveloped Timnit in a warm hug. "Anytime. And I mean that. Call me whenever you need to talk, or even just to sit quietly together."

Timnit's smile was soft but genuine as they parted ways.

As Patricia watched Timnit leave, her unease deepened. Gryoti's secrets were unraveling, but with each new thread, the danger grew.

CHAPTER 14

*P*atricia had lost track of time while consoling Timnit, and there was no way to get her day back on track. With no time to fix dinner, she texted Trey, suggesting they go out. He replied with a suggestion they stay home and have a light dinner of cheese and wine, which suited Patricia perfectly. She removed three blocks of cheese from the refrigerator and set them out on the counter to warm to room temperature.

The kitchen, with its original wide-plank floors, seemed to echo the history of countless meals and conversations that had taken place there. Patricia often found solace in her home, as if its weathered walls whispered reassurances that perseverance could stand the test of time.

When Trey arrived home shortly after five, the creak of the front hall announced his presence. Patricia greeted him warmly as he entered the kitchen.

"How was your day?" she asked.

"It was quite interesting," Trey said, heading to the study, a room lined with floor-to-ceiling bookshelves and the faint scent of aged leather. "Would you care for some wine?"

She nodded.

Trey held a wine bottle up. "Cabernet?"

She nodded again.

While Trey poured the wine in the study, she returned to the kitchen, assembling a plate of cheeses on a slate serving tray. Setting the tray down on the glass-topped kitchen table, she added freshly baked bread from a local market and arranged two sets of polished silver flatware on linen napkins.

Trey entered, glasses of wine in hand, and joined her at the kitchen table. They sat as the setting sun cast a warm, amber glow across the room.

Patricia swirled her wine, inhaled its bouquet, and took a sip, letting it linger on her tongue for a moment. "Delicious," she pronounced.

"I checked on those cases you gave me," Trey said, sampling his wine.

Her heart quickened at the prospect of good news.

"Gryoti used the same lawyer in each case, a guy who is based out of state but licensed to practice in Georgia. All the case files are sealed, so there's no way to get the names of plaintiffs nor witnesses nor any of the evidence against Gryoti." He shook his head. "It's extremely unusual, but it is what it is. I'm sorry, Patsy. It's a total dead end."

Deflated but not defeated, she steeled herself. "Not your fault." She recalled the ill-fated dumpster dive. "He seems to be good at covering his tracks."

"As good as he seems to be, he's not perfect. No one is. And with your thoroughness, when he makes a mistake, you'll catch it."

Patricia gazed at the flame of the single beeswax candle she had lit on the table. Its soft, steady flicker felt like a metaphor for her determination—small but unwavering. "I appreciate your confidence."

He smiled. "I spoke with most of my defense lawyer friends. None have represented Gryoti. None speak negatively of him, and a couple are very positive about the man and his medical practice."

"How can a man so evil be so well thought of?" She leaned back in her chair, letting her eyes drift to the ornate plaster medallion on the ceiling, a relic of another time. "He's killing people. And he's getting away with it." She looked to him for an answer.

Trey appeared deep in thought for a moment. "Technically, so far he hasn't been convicted of violating the law. But that doesn't mean what he is doing is morally justified."

Patricia swirled the wine in her glass again. "That's what's so frustrating. The law is supposed to uphold justice, isn't it? Yet here we are, knowing someone is causing harm but unable to prove it because of legal loopholes. Those sealed cases feel like a betrayal."

Trey nodded. "Or a payoff. The law isn't perfect. It reflects society's attempts to create order, not a perfect moral compass. It's a tool—useful but flawed."

"It's more than that, though," she said, her voice edged with resolve. "People like Gryoti exploit the gaps between moral and legal justice. They act in ways that might not technically break the law but leave a trail of destruction behind them. It's as if he's weaponized the law's limitations."

Trey reached across the table, placing his hand over hers. "That's where people like you come in. The law doesn't always see the whole picture, but you do. You're fighting for something bigger than just rules; you're fighting for what's right. That matters."

Her lips curved into a faint smile. "I just wish I knew how to balance it all. Every time I try to align moral and legal justice, it feels like one step forward and two steps back."

"Keep stepping forward," Trey said gently. "The law may

be rigid, but people like Gryoti make mistakes. And when they do, you'll be there to catch them."

Her resolve hardened. "You're right. No matter how crafty he is, he's not invincible. And I won't stop until I bring him to justice—moral and legal."

Trey gave her hand a reassuring squeeze before releasing it. "Let's dig into that cheese."

AN HOUR LATER, AS PATRICIA WAS CLEANING UP THE KITCHEN, Sheila called.

"My friend Celeste would be happy to talk with you. Do you have a pen handy?"

Patricia grabbed a pen and the notepad she kept in the kitchen. "Got it." She jotted down the phone number Sheila gave her. "When would be the best time to contact her?"

"She said anytime. I have the feeling she wants to vent."

CHAPTER 15

*P*atricia was sitting at her desk that following morning when Willie called.

"Good morning, Patricia. How are you?"

"I'm fine. How about you?"

"I'm finer than a frog's hair split four ways," he said. "I just got off the phone with Dr. Gryoti. He's agreed to be interviewed for a featured article. Matter of fact, he sounded quite excited about the opportunity."

"That's great, Willie. Do you have it scheduled yet?"

"He's a busy guy. We're looking at sometime next week, but we don't have it nailed down yet."

"I can't wait to hear what you come up with."

"I'll let you know as soon as it's completed. How's your investigation going?"

"I have another whistleblower identified through a mutual friend who has agreed to talk with me. My friend says the source is eager to vent."

"I'm happy for you. Just be careful to build trust with your source before asking questions. And when you do get down to business, make sure you ask open-ended questions. With a cooperative source, you can always come back for a second interview for additional details."

"I appreciate your advice."

"Good luck, Patricia."

After talking with Willie, Patricia made an appointment to meet with Celeste the following morning, then began preparing for her lunch meeting with Elena Gryoti, Dr. Gryoti's ex-wife, and then a dissatisfied patient later that afternoon.

Seeking to better understand what patients go through, Patricia did a deep dive on cancer treatments. She couldn't stop scrolling through the articles. The testimonials, the survival rates, the side effects of treatments—they all blurred together in a relentless tide of information. She told herself it was for the case, but the deeper she dove, the harder it became to separate her professional preparation from her personal fears.

The statistics startled her: one in three people were diagnosed with cancer in their lifetime. She lingered over the words "silent killer," feeling them settle like lead in her chest. The thought hit her uninvited: what if cancer was already inside her?

Patricia ran her fingers through her hair, pausing at her temple where a headache had started to throb. Stress, she told herself. She hadn't slept well in days. But lately, every small ache and twinge felt like a warning. She glanced at Trey's photo on her desk. His easy smile, frozen in time, was suddenly tinged with fragility.

She pressed her palm to her chest as her breathing grew shallow. "Stop," she whispered to herself. But the voice in her head refused to quiet: What if Trey had cancer? What if we both did, and we just didn't know it yet?

She closed the laptop with trembling hands. The investigation file lay beside it, thick and accusing. She'd always internalized her cases—every tragedy, every loss. It was why she was so good at her job. But this time, it felt different. This time, it felt personal.

Patricia pushed herself up from the chair and crossed to the window. She wrapped her arms around herself. "Should I get a checkup?" she murmured to the empty room. "But what if…" She swallowed hard. The words refused to come out.

The anxiety was like a living thing, curling around her ribcage and refusing to let go. She closed her eyes. A deep breath. Then another.

Finally, she turned back to the file she hadn't had the heart to put away. "One step at a time," she whispered. For now, that was all she could manage.

She went to the kitchen, hoping to shake her worry. It was good to be moving. She bypassed the coffee pot, removed a can of lemon-flavored seltzer from the icebox, and sat at the kitchen table facing the backyard. She took a sip, savoring the tart lemon, and rested her eyes on the beautiful landscaping glistening in the morning sun.

One of the feral cats, the gray one, sat in the sun, obviously enjoying the warmth. Soon the cat would be roaming freely in the balmier afternoon weather.

PATRICIA SAT ON THE EDGE OF A LOW-SLUNG LEATHER CHAIR, her notebook resting on her knee, pen poised. Late-afternoon light spilled through the sheer curtains of Elena Gryoti's downtown Savannah condo, catching on the polished chrome and glass surfaces. Everything in the room felt expensive, deliberate. A carefully arranged life built after demolition.

Elena stood at the window, back to her guest, a crystal tumbler of bourbon in one hand. She was tall, composed, and beautiful in the way women learn to weaponize after being overlooked for too long. When she finally turned, there was no preamble.

"I'll save you the suspense," she said. "Yes, I know Demetrius was up to something. No, I don't know exactly how he pulled it off."

Patricia nodded slightly. "But you believe he was defrauding patients."

"I don't just believe it. I know it." Elena took a sip, her expression hard. "He used to come home—back when he bothered to come home—smelling like antiseptic and smugness. He'd say things like, 'Some people will pay anything if you put it in an IV bag and wrap it in medical jargon.'"

Patricia's pen scratched across the paper. "He actually said that?"

"Verbatim." Elena let out a sharp laugh, more scorn than amusement. "I asked what he meant, and he gave me that look—doctors love that look, don't they? Like you've just asked them how to spell 'oxygen.' He never told me anything concrete. But he was *proud* of it. Whatever *it* was."

"Did you ever see any financial records?"

Elena shook her head, setting her drink down on a nearby table. "He kept all that locked up tighter than his bedside manner. Wouldn't even let me see the mail. Said I worried too much. But I saw the signs. Every time he hooked someone with deep pockets, he bought himself a new watch. By the time I left, he had a drawer full."

"You divorced five years ago?"

She nodded. "Once our daughter moved out, he didn't even pretend to care. He took me to dinner—oysters, of course—and told me we were finished like he was announcing a stock split. No emotion. Just numbers and timing."

Patricia studied her for a moment. "Do you think he's still running the same scheme?"

"If he hasn't been caught, then absolutely. He doesn't do anything for pleasure. No hobbies, no friends. He only lives for his work. And the thrill of getting away with it."

Patricia leaned forward slightly. "Did you ever hear any names? People he worked with? Clinics? Labs?"

"There was one guy," Elena said after a moment. "Vernon. No last name. Demetrius would get real tense whenever he called. Said it meant he was about to 'make a move.' I thought it was drugs at first, but not the street kind. This was white-collar crime in lab coats."

"And you never saw any of the actual logistics?"

"He never trusted me with details. Treated me like I was just set dressing. But I watched. He never kept records in the house, but one night after dinner, I saw him wiping down flash drives with isopropyl alcohol. Like he was sterilizing evidence."

Patricia's eyes narrowed slightly. "Do you still have anything? Anything he might've left behind?"

Elena hesitated, then walked to a drawer built into a sleek sideboard. She opened it slowly and pulled out a small, heavy object—a gold money clip engraved with DG. She tossed it onto the coffee table between them.

"He left that behind. Carried it everywhere. Called it his lucky charm. I kept it because I like the idea that losing it might drive him insane."

Patricia picked it up and turned it over in her hand. "Mind if I hold on to this?"

"Be my guest." Elena poured herself another measure of bourbon. "Maybe it'll bring you luck." She paused, watching Patricia pocket the money clip. Elena's voice lowered, colder now. "And, Patricia?"

Patricia looked up.

"When you bring him down, don't be gentle. He never was."

. . .

WHILE PATRICIA WAS FRESHENING UP FOR HER AFTERNOON meeting, her phone chirped. She glanced at the screen.

"Hello, Timnit. What's up?"

"Just a quick update. I managed to get into Magnum's security system and surveillance cameras this morning. Gryoti keeps eyes on everything that goes on in his clinic, including his office. I'm trying to document exactly how they handle the infusion drugs from arrival to infusion to disposal. It may take a day or two to track the entire process."

"That's great. Let me know when you have the complete process documented."

Patricia arrived at Annabelle Davis's home just after two. The home, just a block from Summer's, was stunning—a brick, two-story antebellum with tall, slender windows, ornate ironwork on the balconies, and a grand staircase leading to the elegant double front doors.

Annabelle greeted Patricia warmly and led her to a sitting room with a soaring ceiling and intricate crown molding. A marble fireplace dominated one wall.

"Would you care for something to drink?" Annabelle asked.

"No, thank you."

Annabelle gestured to an upholstered sofa. "Shall we sit?"

Patricia sat at one end. Annabelle at the other.

"Well, isn't it just the prettiest day we've had all week?" Annabelle gave a polite smile. "I don't know about you, but I was about ready to build an ark after all that rain we had."

Annabelle starting with small talk allowed Patricia to relax. "I know what you mean. My poor hydrangeas looked like they'd been through a hurricane. But Lord knows, we needed it for the garden."

"Amen to that! And did you catch the sunrise this morning? Just painted the sky like a postcard."

Though small talk was foreign to Patricia, who was usually more direct, she resisted the urge to move prematurely to business. "Oh, I sure did. It reminded me of one of those old summer mornings when the air's just crisp enough to enjoy your coffee on the porch."

"Speaking of coffee, have you been by that new café downtown? Heard they've got the best pecan pie this side of the Mississippi."

Patricia adjusted her body on the comfortable sofa. "No, but I've been meaning to. You'll have to let me know if it's better than Miss June's recipe—though I'm not sure that's possible."

"Ha! We'd have to taste test just to be sure," Annabelle said. "Now, sweetie, what was it you wanted to talk about today?"

"As I mentioned on the phone, I noticed you left a negative review for Magnum Oncology. My mother has been diagnosed with cancer, and because Magnum Oncology is so well regarded, we are considering going there. But you didn't have a good experience, and I wondered if you would mind telling me about it."

"Oh, sweetie, I'd love to, but I can't."

"I'd hate for my mother to have a similar experience. Are you sure you don't want to share?"

"I can't. I signed a non-disclosure agreement."

"Dr. Gryoti had you sign an NDA?"

"No, his attorney did."

"If you don't mind, what was the attorney's name?"

Annabelle thought for a moment. "Judy. Judy something."

According to Trey, Gryoti only had one lawyer, and he was a guy.

"What did she look like?"

"Tall. Beautiful. Very beautiful."

Patricia startled. Could it be Judy Simpson? The woman who had killed her mother. The woman Patricia had shot in self-defense. The woman the police couldn't find. But Judy wasn't an attorney. To be sure, Patricia asked, "Did she have a hand injury? Right hand?"

"I don't believe so."

Judy could have had her hand reconstructed. "Red hair?"

"No, blonde. And beautiful blue eyes."

The lawyer who visited Annabelle probably wasn't Judy, the woman who had murdered her mother and fled. It wouldn't make sense for her to stick around in Savannah where she was so well-known given she was a murderer with an active warrant. And, if she was in Savannah, she wouldn't use her real name. No, the attorney wasn't Judy Simpson.

CHAPTER 16

The following morning, Patricia stood outside a modest yet cozy-looking condo, its exterior marked by tidy flower boxes and a welcome mat that read, *Come in for Tea.* She adjusted her jacket against the breeze and knocked on the door. Moments later, it swung open to reveal Celeste Wright, her auburn hair loosely tied back and an oversized cardigan draped over her shoulders.

"Patricia?" Celeste asked, a tentative smile forming.

"That's me," Patricia replied warmly, extending her hand. "Thank you so much for agreeing to meet with me. Sheila said you were incredibly kind, and I'm grateful you're willing to talk."

Celeste shook her hand and stepped aside. "Any friend of Sheila's is a friend of mine. Come on in—sorry for the mess."

The condo was anything but messy. The living room had a comforting air, with soft lighting, a plush couch, and shelves lined with books and small potted plants. A faint herbal scent lingered in the air.

"Make yourself comfortable," Celeste said, gesturing to

the couch. "Would you like some tea? I just brewed a chamomile blend."

"Tea sounds perfect, thank you," Patricia said, setting her bag by her feet and settling on to the couch.

Celeste disappeared into the kitchen and returned moments later with two mugs. She handed one to Patricia before sitting in an armchair across from her.

"Sheila mentioned you're looking into Dr. Gryoti's business," Celeste said, her voice soft but weighted with something unspoken.

Patricia wrapped her hands around the warm mug, nodding gently. A ribbon of steam curled upward from the mug, carrying the rich scent of roasted beans. "She said you used to work with him at Magnum Oncology." She paused, her tone careful but open. "I wasn't sure if you'd want to talk about it, but I really appreciate you meeting with me."

Celeste tilted her head, her expression clouding as she considered Patricia's words. Finally, she let out a quiet sigh. "I'll be honest, it's not an easy topic for me. Gryoti is… well, he's brilliant, there's no denying that. Charismatic too. But there's another side to him. A side I couldn't ignore forever."

Patricia stayed quiet for a moment, letting Celeste gather her thoughts. "I'm listening," she said gently. "Take your time."

Celeste stared down at her own mug, running her thumb along the rim. "When I first started at Magnum, his work seemed groundbreaking, almost revolutionary. He'd talk about this new class of pharmaceuticals he was developing, treatments he claimed could slow the progress of certain hard to control cancers. It all sounded so promising." Her voice faltered slightly before she continued. "But then things started to feel off."

Patricia leaned in slightly. "What do you mean?"

Celeste glanced up, her expression tightening. "He always

said we were in the early human trial phase. But those trials weren't being conducted through any official channels. He was only offering his so-called treatments to wealthy patients; the kind of people who could afford to pay obscene amounts of money for a shot at something unproven."

Patricia's eyes narrowed. "And they went along with it?"

"Some did, some didn't. The ones who hesitated? He had a way of pushing them. Hard. He'd tell them, flat out, 'Without my treatments, you're going to die.' I heard him say it more than once."

Patricia exhaled slowly, her jaw tightening. "That's manipulative, and unethical."

"That's just the start." Celeste's voice dropped, growing more strained. "No one—not the other doctors, or the nurses, not even the patients—was allowed to see the full treatment records. Everything was fragmented. Gryoti made sure every piece of the process was compartmentalized so no one really understood the full picture. Except him."

Patricia's stomach churned as she absorbed Celeste's words. "Do you know anything about the drugs he was using? Where they came from?"

Celeste hesitated, her fingers tightening around her mug. "That's another thing. Gryoti was obsessed with secrecy. The drugs just appeared. And anything related to the treatments —empty vials, packaging, even syringes—had to be disposed of in a special locked bin in his office. He claimed it was to protect his research, but honestly? It felt like he was hiding something."

A grim silence settled between them. Patricia's mind raced as she tried to piece it all together. "Did anyone ever confront him about any of this?"

Celeste shook her head slowly. "Not openly. We all knew he was untouchable. And those who dared to even hint at suspicions… let's just say he had a way of shutting them down before they could do anything about it. That's why I left. I couldn't keep looking the other way."

Patricia leaned back, her eyes searching Celeste's face. "You've been carrying this for a long time," she said quietly. "Thank you for trusting me with it."

A flicker of a smile crossed Celeste's lips, though her eyes were still heavy with worry. "If there's even a chance you can stop him, it's worth speaking up. Just be careful. Gryoti's not the kind of man who'll let anyone expose him without a fight."

Patricia's expression hardened; her determination clear. "I'll keep that in mind," she said firmly. "And don't worry, I'm not afraid of a fight."

That afternoon, Patricia paced anxiously in her kitchen, her fingers gripping her phone tightly as she watched two Chatham Police officers pack her laptop into an evidence bag. Their arrival had been sudden, a sharp knock at the door followed by a warrant for her laptop. They claimed she had hacked into Magnum Oncology's computer network. The accusation was absurd—she didn't even know how to code. But Simon and Timnit did. Her stomach churned at the thought of what might have gone wrong.

"This is a mistake," she said, trying to keep her voice steady. "I haven't hacked anyone's network. You'll see there's nothing on that laptop."

The taller of the two officers, a man with a thin mustache and a stern expression, didn't look up. "Ma'am, we're just following protocol. The warrant gives us the authority to seize this device. If you have any objections, you can raise them with the court."

Patricia bit back a sharp reply, knowing it would do her no good. She watched as they sealed the evidence bag, left an inventory sheet, and exited the house. The door clicked shut behind them, leaving a suffocating silence in their wake.

Her first thought was to call Simon, but she dismissed it just as quickly. Any communication with him now could look incriminating. Instead, she scrolled through her contacts and hit Trey's number. Her husband's calm, measured voice answered on the second ring.

"Trey, it's me," she said, her voice shaking. "The police were just here. They took my laptop. They think I hacked Magnum Oncology."

There was a pause on the other end of the line before Trey responded. "What? Did they show you a warrant?"

"Yes," she said, eyeing the warrant on the counter. "They said it's evidence, but I didn't do anything. Trey, you have to help me."

"Of course," Trey said firmly. "Don't say anything to anyone else. I'll be there in twenty minutes. We'll get this sorted out."

True to his word, Trey arrived within twenty minutes, a determined expression on his face. He gave Patricia's shoulder a reassuring squeeze before setting to work.

An hour later, Trey walked briskly into the Chatham Police headquarters, his suit perfectly pressed and briefcase in hand. His expression was that of a man who didn't take no for an answer.

At the front desk, an officer looked up, startled by his abrupt arrival. "Can I help you?" the officer asked.

"I'm Trey Falcon, attorney. I'm here regarding the unlawful seizure of my client Patricia Falcon's property. Specifically, her laptop," Trey said, his voice firm and professional. "I need to speak with whoever signed off on the warrant."

The officer hesitated before nodding. "Wait here. I'll get Detective Monroe."

A few minutes later, Detective Monroe appeared, her face lined with skepticism. Trey wasted no time.

"Detective Monroe, I'd like to see the affidavit supporting the warrant," Trey demanded. "I have reason to believe the seizure of my client's laptop was based on insufficient evidence and violates her constitutional rights."

Detective Monroe's jaw tightened. "The warrant was signed by a judge. It's all above board."

Trey placed his briefcase on the counter and opened it, retrieving a stack of legal documents. "I'm not here to debate the warrant's validity in theory. I'm here to request the immediate return of that laptop. It contains privileged communications, including legally protected materials. Any access to that data would constitute a breach of attorney-client confidentiality."

Monroe crossed her arms. "The laptop is evidence in a cybercrime investigation."

"Again Detective, as her attorney, I am invoking her rights under the law, including but not limited to that of attorney client confidentiality," Trey countered. "If you insist on keeping that laptop, we'll see each other in court tomorrow morning when I file a motion to suppress the evidence and for injunctive relief."

Monroe studied him for a long moment, then sighed. "Wait here."

TREY HAD BEEN GONE FOR TWO HOURS, WHEN THE KITCHEN door swung open and Trey walked in, laptop in hand. Patricia, who had been sitting at the kitchen table, jumped to her feet.

"You got it back!" she exclaimed, relief flooding her voice.

Trey held up a hand to stop her. "Yes, but we're not out of the woods yet. The police are watching you, Patricia. You need to be extremely careful about what you say and do from now on."

"I didn't hack anything," Patricia said, her voice shaking.

"I know," Trey said, putting the laptop down on the kitchen table. "But you need to tell me everything—every detail about Simon, Timnit, Magnum, and what's been going on. Nothing held back, Patsy. We need a defense, and we need it now."

She nodded, her eyes wide. "Of course. I'll tell you everything."

"And from now on," Trey said, looking her squarely in the eyes, "we fight smart."

Patricia swallowed hard, her mind already racing to piece together the facts that would keep her out of Gryoti's legal crosshairs.

CHAPTER 17

Night cloaked the city. At Magnum Oncology, in the private quarters he rarely visited, Dr. Gryoti stood beside a glowing fireplace.

The room was sparce, monastic, except for the desk—oak and imposing—and the built-in safe behind a Camargue landscape. He opened it, removed a small flash drive, and handed it to Carol.

"She's logging everything about us," he said. "Timelines. Contacts. I want that data."

Carol turned the drive over. "Her laptop's not vulnerable."

"Then create the vulnerability. Have Judy get into it. Plant the drive. Make it look like curiosity."

He turned and stared out at the city. Savannah glittered, unaware.

"No direct line to me," he added.

Carol hesitated. "We're not dealing with amateurs."

"Neither are they."

He sat. On his desk, Naomi's photo smiled up at him, mid-performance, alive in the music.

"I built this for her," he said, half to himself. "Not just a clinic. Not just money. A legacy. A monument."

Carol watched him carefully.

"And Patricia Falcon wants to tear it down." His voice dropped to a whisper. "We'll see who's still standing."

CHAPTER 18

The hum of the Sentient Bean coffee shop blended with the rhythmic clinking of spoons against ceramic cups. Timnit sat across from Patricia. Her dark-brown eyes, usually sharp and decisive, were clouded with uncertainty. Patricia leaned forward, her blonde hair catching the morning light, her gaze soft but attentive.

"So what's the verdict?" Patricia asked, setting her chai latte down. "You've been chewing on this for days."

"First off, the Triple Canopy is totally legit. No connection to Gryoti." Timnit sighed, the sound heavy with the weight of her thoughts. "And they're offering me more money than I've ever seen in one place. Full benefits, relocation package if I want it, and a leadership role. It's everything someone with my background should want."

Patricia's lips twitched. "But?"

"But it's not what I need," Timnit admitted. She looked down at her hands, calloused from years of military training, then back at Patricia. "Savannah, this place, it's home now. And working with you? It's given me a sense of purpose I didn't even know I was missing."

Patricia tilted her head, her expression thoughtful. "Timnit, I'll be the first to admit your skills are beyond anything I could ever dream of having. But you don't owe me anything. You don't owe Savannah anything. If this job is what's best for you and David, you should take it."

Timnit smiled faintly. "David's been supportive, of course. Told me to do what feels right, but he's overseas. He doesn't see the day-to-day here. The local crime, the families torn apart by scams and fraud and outright evil. If I don't stay and help, who will? The police have their hands full, and not many people around here have the kind of training I do."

Patricia reached across the table and placed a hand over Timnit's. "It's not just about skills. It's about where your heart is. If bringing justice to this city means more to you than the paycheck, then you've already made your decision."

Timnit's eyes glistened as she chuckled softly. "When you say it like that, it sounds so simple."

"Sometimes the simplest truths are the hardest to face," Patricia said with a wink. "You've got a moral compass that would make most people jealous. Trust it."

Timnit leaned back in her chair. "I called them this morning. Told them no."

Patricia raised an eyebrow. "And you didn't tell me until now?"

Timnit shrugged. "I wanted to see if you'd try to convince me to stay."

"You didn't need convincing. You needed clarity, And maybe a good cup of coffee." Patricia's smile dimmed slightly. "Speaking of clarity, there's something I need to tell you. The police seized my laptop. They're accusing me of hacking Magnum Oncology's network."

Timnit straightened, her expression sharpening. "What? Are you serious? What evidence do they have?"

"They claim the breach was traced back to my IP address.

It's ridiculous, of course, but there's going to be a fight to clear my name," Patricia said, her tone edged with frustration. "I wanted to warn you, though. You've accessed their security systems and cameras. If they find out, it could get messy."

Timnit's jaw tightened. "We need to insulate ourselves from this. First, I'll wipe all traces of activity from the systems I've touched. Second, I'll set up a secure channel for anything related to Magnum so it can't be traced back to us."

"Good," Patricia said with a nod. "And let's keep everything on encrypted drives from now on. No more direct connections."

Timnit's lips quirked into a smile. "Looks like it's a good thing I'm not going anywhere. We've got work to do."

"We always do," Patricia replied, her smile returning despite the gravity of the situation. "But we'll get through this. Together."

They clinked their mugs, the weight of their shared mission settling between them.

THE SOFT GLOW OF THE RESTAURANT DINING ROOM LIGHT bathed their table in a warm, golden hue. Patricia sat across from Trey. His tie was loosened, his sleeves rolled up. He looked tired but content, a smile playing on his lips as he recounted a lighter moment from his day in court. His voice was a balm for Patricia's frayed nerves.

She tried to focus on his words, but her mind kept wandering—to the threatening email, to the relentless hours she'd spent digging into Gryoti's records, and to the dull ache in her chest she couldn't quite ignore anymore. She glanced at Trey, his blue eyes sparkling as he chuckled at his own anecdote. She loved that laugh, that spark. It was why she'd fallen for him all those years ago in law school.

"Penny for your thoughts?" Trey's voice broke through her reverie.

She smiled. "Just thinking about how much I miss you."

He leaned forward, concern flickering across his face. "I'm right here."

"I know," she said, reaching across the table to take his hand. His palm was warm, grounding her. "But we're always so busy. You with the firm, me with my projects. When was the last time we really spent time together? Just us."

Trey tilted his head, considering. "Are you saying my dazzling company at dinner isn't enough?"

She laughed softly. "I'm saying we need a real break. A vacation. Just you and me."

Trey's smile faded slightly, replaced by a thoughtful frown. "A vacation," he echoed, almost as if testing the word.

"Yes," Patricia said, her voice gaining strength. "We've never done it. Not even with Hayley, really. And now she's off at college, and it feels like time is slipping away. I don't want us to wake up one day and realize we've spent our whole lives working, never just being together."

Trey's eyes softened. "I get it. Believe me, I do. I'd love nothing more than to whisk you away to some quiet beach and just… be. No emails, no clients, no cases."

"So let's do it," she pressed, hope flickering in her chest.

He sighed, leaning back in his chair. "It's not that simple, Patsy. The firm's busier than ever, and I've got two major trials coming up."

"I understand," she said quickly, though the disappointment in her voice was hard to hide. "It's just I'm tired, Trey. Tired of running myself ragged, of…" She trailed off, unable to voice the deeper worries gnawing at her.

Trey reached across the table again, his hand covering hers. "You've been carrying a lot lately, haven't you?"

She nodded, tears pricking at the corners of her eyes. "I don't want to keep carrying it alone."

He squeezed her hand. "You're not alone, Patsy. You never are. Look, maybe we can't take that trip right now, but we'll make it happen. Next year, when things settle down. And in the meantime, we can carve out time here. Date nights, weekends, whatever you need."

She smiled through the tears that threatened to spill over. "You mean it?"

"Of course," he said. "You're my priority, Patsy. Always."

She let out a shaky breath, the knot in her chest loosening slightly. "Thank you."

He smiled, leaning over the table to kiss her hand. "Anything for you."

For the first time in weeks, Patricia felt a glimmer of peace. They might not have all the time in the world, but they had each other. And for now, that was enough.

CHAPTER 19

A morning chill seeped through the old windowpanes in the kitchen, a gentle reminder to Patricia that even in the South, autumn finds its way. Outside, a fine mist hung in the air, clinging to the Spanish moss that draped the backyard live oak like spectral lace. Inside, the lingering aroma of Trey's strong coffee mingled with the scent of the bacon she had fried for him, a comforting contrast to the damp chill seeping in.

After cleaning up the dishes and feeding the feral cats, Patricia headed upstairs, jogged on the treadmill, then took a long, warm shower. She dressed in faded jeans and a thick cable knit sweater, went back downstairs, and poured a thermal mug of steaming coffee.

Now, with her routine complete, it was time to return to the task at hand, the unsettling puzzle of Gryoti and the fact that his pristine medical practice was nothing more than a carefully constructed façade. She went into the study, placed the mug on a coaster next to her laptop, and sat at the desk. Steam rose from the mug, slow and hypnotic.

A sudden, insistent chime from her phone shattered the quiet of the study. *Meredith*, the screen flashed.

"Hello, Meredith. What's up?" Patricia asked, her voice tighter than she intended.

"Just an update," Meredith said. "I've uncovered evidence that, in addition to making substantial contributions to local politicians, Gryoti is providing kickbacks to local physicians who refer patients to him."

"Illegal?" Patricia's grip on her phone tightened. The coffee sat untouched, its steam no longer a comfort but a mocking reminder of time lost.

"Absolutely," Meredith said, the word heavy with implications. "But there's more. Gryoti is making huge contributions to fake charities."

"Also illegal?" Patricia's gaze darted around the room, as if expecting Gryoti himself to materialize from the shadows.

"Yes, indeed. The amount is staggering. Looks like money laundering. It appears he's doing this for tax evasion."

Patricia's pen scratched frantically across her notepad, the sound amplified in the tense silence of the room. "Thanks, Meredith. Put the evidence into an encrypted file unrelated to you. Don't use our usual protocols."

"Okay." The rapid, staccato clicks of keys from Meredith's end sounded like an approaching threat. "Done. Why encrypt the evidence?"

"Somehow Gryoti's lawyer filed a warrant that convinced the authorities I had hacked Magnum's network, and, consequently, they seized my laptop. Trey got it back just before they could search it, but Gryoti is clearly escalating." She paused, the unspoken dread filling the space. "Encrypt everything, anything that can even remotely tie you to it, and cover your tracks. Assume Gryoti is watching."

"Thanks for the heads-up. I'll get right on it. Stay safe."

After hanging up, Patricia's gaze swept across the study;

the stack of antique books on the shelves seemed to judge her from their silent positions, and the worn leather of her chair felt cold against her back. Her hand shook slightly as she dialed Ellery, the dial tone sounding like a warning. She told her about the threatening note and the laptop seizure, the words catching in her throat.

"I'm not surprised," Ellery said, her voice sharp. "He's clever and well-connected, and now he's feeling cornered. Document everything, *everything*, you find, before he destroys the evidence. Create a case file and keep everything there, meticulously organized."

"I already have a thorough case file," Patricia said. "It's a chronological log of everything I do and find."

"Good. Now make a copy, keep the copy up to date, and keep both copies offline. Assume his reach is farther than you think."

"Okay."

"Where is the threatening note you received?"

"In a sealed envelope in my desk." Patricia took a sip of the cooling coffee, the taste acrid and unwelcome.

"Does your husband have a safe at his office?"

"Yes. And we have a walk-in safe at home."

"A home walk-in. That's impressive, but I think your home safe could become compromised. Don't forget, he was able to get a warrant for your laptop. If he can do that, he can probably manufacture a reason to get a warrant to get inside your home safe. Keep your physical evidence somewhere else entirely, not in your house."

"Okay." Patricia felt a chill crawl down her spine.

Ellery's voice was clipped and urgent as she outlined how to handle, label, and safely keep evidence. "Seal evidence in appropriate containers, label them with your name, when it was obtained, and where from. You need to be able to prove a rock-solid chain of custody."

"Only one piece of physical evidence so far, the note," Patricia said.

"Speaking of which, you should get a sample of Gryoti's handwriting to compare to the handwriting on that note."

Patricia added it to her to-do list, her movements quick and frantic. "We took a look at Gryoti's trash. Found nothing. Not a shred of evidence of the drugs."

"That was a good idea to search his trash. Risky, but good. If you had found drug evidence, it would have probably required a special evidence container and refrigeration to preserve it. I suggest you prepare an evidence kit. Be ready for anything. I'll text you a list for an evidence kit and the contact information for a supplier. Get it today."

"Thank you. This is all so helpful."

"And never forget to always use gloves to avoid contaminating evidence."

The coffee in her stomach churned, a sickly feeling mixed with the adrenaline that was coursing through her veins. "Oh no. I didn't use gloves when I handled the note."

"Don't worry, it can't be undone now. Just get a box or two of gloves and keep them in your car, your purse, everywhere. And from now on, be meticulous about using them. You're playing a dangerous game, Patricia. Be smart."

When the call was completed, Patricia sat back in her chair, her breath coming in shallow, ragged gasps. Her gaze darted towards the window, the familiar scene of Falcon Square now feeling like a hostile landscape. The ancient oaks seemed to loom, their branches twisted like claws. She had so much to learn, so much to fear, and the crushing weight of the task before her made it clear she was now playing a very dangerous game, where one wrong move could end it all.

She needed to stay smart, grounded, and reel in her emotions. A quick call to Summer resulted in an invitation for an immediate face to face.

Patricia spread out a series of documents, photos, and printouts on the coffee table in Summer's sitting room. The room, always imbued with warmth from its rich wood tones and soft lamplight, now had an air of quiet urgency. Summer, seated cross-legged on the couch, leaned forward with sharp focus.

"Alright," Summer said, "let's see what we have here." She reached for one of the documents, her fine-boned hands deftly flipping through the pages. "You said Gryoti's got politicians, medical board officials, and whistleblowers all tangled in his web?"

"That's what Meredith's forensic accounting is suggesting," Patricia replied. She tapped on a flowchart she'd sketched on a notepad. "We know he's been making hefty campaign donations, and there are whispers of kickbacks to doctors who send patients his way, but we haven't pinned down the specifics."

Summer scanned the chart. "Hmm. Look here," she said, pointing to the relationship map, a cluster of names linked by arrows. "This isn't random. He's operating like a classic organized crime network. The politicians provide cover, the doctors funnel in the patients, and the medical board looks the other way. Gryoti's at the center, but he's insulated himself with layers of plausible deniability."

"How do we crack it?" Patricia asked.

Summer leaned back, her delicate fingers steepled. "We start by looking for pressure points. Every network like this has weak links. People who feel undervalued, wronged, or who simply have a conscience. And Gryoti's overconfidence might be another crack in his armor. Narcissists tend to overestimate the loyalty of their underlings."

Patricia's lips pressed into a thin line. "I've spoken to a few disgruntled former employees, but most of them are too scared to say much. They've all mentioned intimidation—threats, NDAs, and mysterious accidents."

Summer's expression darkened. "Classic tactics. Fear is his greatest weapon. But it also means there's someone—or multiple someones—tasked with enforcing that fear. If we can identify who's carrying out the dirty work, we can find a way in."

"You think it's one of these people?" Patricia gestured to Simon's relationship map of Gryoti.

Summer tilted her head, considering. "Maybe. Or maybe it's someone on the periphery. Look at his financial interactions. Follow the money. It'll lead you to the enforcers, the bribed officials, and the whistleblowers who've been silenced."

Patricia nodded, making a note. "Meredith's already working on tracking his financials. But if we could connect his donations to specific political favors or medical board decisions..."

"That would be gold," Summer agreed. "And don't discount social connections. Narcissists like Gryoti love to flaunt their power. If we dig into his appearances at galas, fundraisers, or even high-profile personal gatherings, we might spot patterns, like which politicians or doctors he's closest to. Those are the people most likely to know his secrets."

Patricia's eyes lit up. "I've got photos from that gala Trey and I attended. Gryoti was schmoozing with all kinds of people. Timnit ran facial recognition on the photos."

Summer smiled. "Good. Once you have names, cross-reference them with the money trail and see who pops up in both places. And keep an eye out for inconsistencies—people who've suddenly come into money or who've made decisions that don't align with their usual behavior."

"You really think we can unravel this?" Patricia asked, her tone a mix of hope and doubt.

Summer reached out and placed a reassuring hand on Patricia's arm. "It won't be easy, but every web has a weak thread. Find it, tug it, and the whole thing will come undone. You've already got the determination. Now we just need to keep digging."

Patricia smiled, bolstered by Summer's confidence. "Alright. Let's get to work."

The two women bent over the documents, their combined skills weaving together a strategy to dismantle Gryoti's sprawling network piece by piece. Outside, the Savannah evening settled in, but inside, the resolve to bring justice burned brightly.

CHAPTER 20

*P*atricia glanced at her watch as it vibrated gently, the chime breaking the heavy silence of the room. The notification glowed ominously: a reminder of her committee meeting at Falcon Hospital. "Great," she muttered, the word clipped. Too much to do, too little time.

She closed her laptop with a decisive snap, the screen going black as if mirroring the frustration creeping over her. Rising from her office chair, she moved toward the front closet. Her fingers hesitated as she sifted through the neatly hung coats. Should she skip the meeting and get back to the investigation? No. The hospital needed her as much as the investigation did. She finally grabbed a lightweight vest, sliding it on with automatic precision. Adjusting the zipper, she exhaled slowly, her thoughts flickering between the hospital meeting agenda and her investigative to-do list. Shaking it off, she grabbed her handbag and made her way toward the garage.

The air in the garage was cooler, tinged with the sharp scent of motor oil and rubber. Patricia flipped the light switch, bathing the space in a stark, fluorescent glow. Her gaze landed on her car—a sleek black Navigator gleaming under the harsh lights. She allowed herself a smile, comforted by its sturdy, familiar presence. But as she stepped closer, her smile faltered, replaced by a sinking dread.

"What the—" Her voice pierced the stillness, sharp and disbelieving. She froze in place, staring at the vehicle.

Both left tires were flat, their rubber sagging in defeated, crumpled folds against the concrete floor. A faint metallic smell reached her nose, mingling with the cool air in a way that made her stomach twist. A check of the right showed both tires on that side were also flat. This wasn't wear and tear, it wasn't bad luck. This was deliberate.

Her hands trembled slightly as she pulled out her phone. Dialing quickly, she forced her voice into an even tone. "Hi, this is Patricia. I won't be able to make the meeting today—car trouble. Sorry for the short notice." She ended the call, her lips pressed into a thin line. Without pausing, she dialed another number.

"Hi, I need to get my car to the dealership," she said when the AAA operator answered. "I have four flat tires." Her voice was steady, but her eyes darted to the tires again. A chill crept up her spine, raising the fine hairs on her arms.

At the dealership, Patricia paced the waiting area, her heels digging into the carpet. The room was too warm. The TV too loud. Her reflection stared back at her from the glass separating the waiting room from the repair bays, her face pale and drawn. She barely recognized herself.

Finally, the service manager emerged, his face smudged with grease and his expression unreadable. In one hand, he held her fob. In the other, a small plastic bag.

"Your car's ready," he said, but there was something in his tone, an edge of unease. He handed her the fob. "We found these." He held up the bag, revealing its contents: four nails, their jagged points catching the fluorescent light.

Patricia's stomach churned. Her fingers tightened around the bag. "Someone left these in my tires?" Her voice wavered slightly.

"That's what it looks like. You might want to keep an eye on your car." The words hung in the air, heavy with implication.

She nodded, muttering a quick thanks. The bag felt heavier than it should as she slipped it into her purse.

Driving home, her grip on the steering wheel was white-knuckled, her heart pounding as her mind spun. This wasn't random. Was it Gryoti? Was he sending me yet another message?

Once home, Patricia dropped her bag on the kitchen counter and headed straight to her office. She powered her laptop on, the soft glow of the screen cutting through the room's shadows. Navigating to the security footage from the garage, she began scrolling through the recordings.

Each frame blurred into the next as her eyes strained against the images. Her pulse quickened every time she thought she saw movement, only to find nothing but shadows shifting with the light. After an hour, she leaned back in frustration. "Nothing," she muttered bitterly.

She pulled the bag of nails from her purse. Sliding it into a large envelope, she placed it carefully in her desk drawer. Her fingers hesitated as they brushed against another envelope—the one containing the anonymous note she'd received earlier. A faint tremor ran through her as she closed the drawer with a soft but definitive click. She had to get the evidence out of the house.

Shortly after five, the front door creaked open, followed by the familiar thud of Trey's shoes against the floor. "Hey, Patsy," he called from the door of her office. "Are you okay? You look tense."

Patricia turned to him. "Someone vandalized my car

today," she said, her voice tight, controlled. "All four tires were flat, and the dealership found nails in them."

Trey's jaw clenched, his brow furrowing deeply. "Do you think it's Gryoti?" he asked.

"I'm almost certain." She crossed her arms. "But there's no evidence. Nothing on the garage cameras." She sighed, the frustration in her voice giving way to exhaustion. She removed both envelopes from the drawer. "Can you store these in your office safe? The note and the nails. They're evidence in my investigation. I want them out of reach of Gryoti and his absurd warrants."

"Of course." His voice was resolute as he tucked the envelopes under his arm. "We'll figure this out."

Over dinner, the atmosphere was heavy, the clink of utensils against plates unusually loud in the silence. Patricia's gaze kept flickering toward the windows, her thoughts racing. The warm light from the chandelier above cast shifting shadows, but instead of comfort, the play of light seemed to magnify her unease.

"We need to make sure this doesn't happen again," she said abruptly, breaking the silence. Her voice was firm, but there was a note of underlying urgency. She looked at Trey, her fork hovering above her plate. "What do you think about asking Simon to upgrade the garage security and surveillance?"

Trey met her eyes. "That makes sense. I'll talk to him tomorrow. He might have ideas for better coverage." His calm tone was meant to reassure, but Patricia could sense the tension in his clipped response.

"Good," she said, nodding with a sharpness that surprised even her. Her fingers tightened around the edge of the table. "I can't let this go unanswered."

Trey didn't reply, instead reaching for his wine glass. The

faint sound of the liquid sloshing as he swirled it filled the space between them.

After dinner, they moved to the family room, carrying their half-empty glasses. Trey knelt by the fireplace, his movements precise as he stacked the logs and lit the kindling. The fire crackled to life, the warm glow illuminating his face as he sat back on his heels, watching the flames catch.

Patricia sank into the sofa, pulling a throw blanket over her legs. She didn't feel the warmth of the fire; the chill she'd been carrying since the discovery in the garage hadn't left her. Trey joined her moments later, settling in beside her. The sofa creaked softly as he leaned back.

"You've had a tough day," he said, his tone gentle but probing.

She nodded, her eyes fixed on the fire. "I'm still disturbed that someone could get into our garage undetected," she said, her voice quieter now but taut, like a wire stretched too thin.

Trey placed an arm around her shoulders, pulling her closer. "We'll fix that." His voice steady, though she could feel tension in the way his fingers lightly squeezed her arm.

Patricia reached for her phone from the end table, the glow of the screen momentarily bright against the dim room. She angled it toward them and snapped a selfie, the faint click joining the crackling of the fire.

Trey turned to her, his brow furrowed. "What's up, Patsy? You don't normally take selfies of us."

"Nothing," she said with a small, forced smile. "I just want to capture this moment." She set the phone aside and leaned into him, the scent of the firewood mingling with his familiar citrus aftershave. "The fire is nice. You're so nice."

"This isn't you," Trey said, his voice soft but firm. "Come on. What's going on?"

Patricia let out a long sigh. Her throat tightened as she

tried to hold back the tears that threatened to spill. "I don't want to lose you," she whispered finally.

He shifted to face her more fully, concern etched into his features. "I'm not going anywhere," he said.

"Ever since your kidnapping," she began, her words trembling, "I've repeatedly worried about losing you. And cancer—you often don't know about it until it's too late. I don't want to lose you." She squeezed his arm. "The data says we're vulnerable."

Trey's face softened, though his eyes remained serious. "So what do you want to do?" he asked.

Patricia drew in a shaky breath. "Let's start with some early detection. I'm already getting mammograms, but I think we should both schedule colonoscopies now, rather than waiting until we turn forty-five. Also, I think we should get blood tests for genetic cancer markers."

He nodded without hesitation. "Sure. Anything else?"

"I think we should update our trusts and wills."

Trey's brow furrowed slightly. "If we do all this, will you feel better?"

"I don't know," Patricia admitted, her voice cracking slightly. "But at least it's a start."

"You realize I already get an annual physical and blood tests every six months?" he asked gently.

She nodded.

"My doctors say I'm healthy," he added.

"I know, Trey. But I can't shake these fears." Her voice wavered as she spoke, and she dropped her gaze, staring at the glass of wine trembling slightly in her hands.

Trey reached over, his hand covering hers. "Well, we'll do what you asked," he said softly. "But I want you to talk to Beau about your concerns about cancer. He might have some additional ideas to help."

She sat up slightly, meeting his gaze, and leaned forward,

pressing a kiss to his cheek. "Thank you for hearing me out on this," she said, her voice steadier now. "It helps. It really does."

Trey pulled her closer, the firelight casting flickering shadows across the room. "We'll figure it out," he said, his voice calm and sure.

But despite his comforting words, she couldn't quite shake the gnawing fear that something—someone—was still lurking in the shadows.

CHAPTER 21

First thing the following morning, Patricia called Beau and arranged to talk with him, then dressed for the day. She adjusted the collar of her soft cable-knit sweater—cream, of course—smoothed her jeans, a rare break from her usual Lilly Pulitzer shifts, then headed downstairs and made tea.

Entering the front parlor of her historic home on Falcon Square, she sat at the desk. The desk bore the patina of age and history, its surface gleaming beneath the morning sun that spilled through tall, lace-curtained windows.

The room smelled faintly of lemon oil from the polished floors and a hint of cinnamon from her mug of tea. Patricia paused a moment, her eyes taking in the scene beyond the window: the quiet square, with its wandering pathways and towering oaks draped in Spanish moss. It was a scene of Southern charm and tradition, a world away from the dark truths she was uncovering.

As she reviewed her case file, her phone vibrated on the desk. She answered the call, her slight drawl wrapping warmly around her words.

"Good mornin', Willie. How are you this fine, beautiful day?"

"Fair to middlin', Patricia. And you?" Willie's easy, Southern cadence came through the speaker.

"If the good Lord's willin' and the creek don't rise, I might finally catch a break in this investigation today," Patricia replied, her voice tinged with determination.

"I might be able to help you with that. I couldn't get Gryoti to incriminate himself in my first interview, but he raised the idea that we write a book together. A memoir. I've got a second interview set up, so we've got another shot at pinning him down. Probably many shots considering how long it'll take to write the book."

"Well, he's a slippery one, but I reckon he's no match for you."

"Thank you kindly," Willie replied, the smile in his voice unmistakable.

CHAPTER 22

After talking with Willie, Patricia called Simon.

"Could you come over sometime and upgrade our garage security? I don't want to have any more unauthorized entries."

"Yes. The garage *is* the weakest point in your security. I'll come over and see what I can do to beef it up. Will you be around today?"

"Yes."

An hour later, Simon stood at her front door.

"That was quick," Patricia said, smiling despite herself as she stepped aside to let him in.

"Efficiency's my specialty," Simon replied, his voice carrying a warmth that softened his otherwise intimidating demeanor.

Patricia led him to the dining room, where he liked to set up his gear. She turned to him as they entered, tilting her head slightly. "Do you need anything before you start?"

He set two large, black duffle bags down, the sound of their weight hitting the floor heavy and solid. He ran a calloused hand through his thick, dark hair, the faintest smirk curling his lips. "If you've got any Black Rifle coffee left, I wouldn't say no."

Patricia chuckled, shaking her head. "I'll make a fresh pot if you can wait."

"Perfect," Simon said, already unzipping one of his duffle bags.

As Patricia moved to the kitchen, the familiar sounds of Simon setting up filled the house—the soft scrapes of metal against wood. It was oddly comforting.

The aroma of freshly brewing coffee soon mingled with the scent of chocolate as she plated two oven-fresh double fudge brownies. She returned to the dining room, placing the plate beside Simon's laptop. He glanced up at her, his eyes momentarily softening, and grabbed a brownie. He took a bite, a smile breaking across his face. "Delicious," he said, the single word thick with appreciation.

"Grandma's secret recipe," Patricia said, a flicker of pride in her voice.

"She has a gift," Simon said. He returned the half-eaten brownie to the plate and leaned forward, his demeanor shifting to serious. "So, first things first—garage security. I'll upgrade your system as much as I can today. I've also ordered some new state-of-the-art components. They should arrive next week. Are you okay with that?"

Patricia leaned against the edge of the table, her arms crossed over her chest. Her eyes locked on Simon's. "It's your show, Simon. Just do what you think is best."

He nodded, expression unreadable, then headed out to the garage.

Patricia's phone buzzed in her pocket as she walked back to her office. The name "Ramona Cortez" flashed on the screen. Curious, she answered.

"I have some information about Magnum that might be

helpful to you," Ramona said without preamble. Her voice was low, hesitant, as if she were afraid of being overheard.

Patricia frowned, her instincts flaring. "What kind of information?"

The conversation quickly turned strange. Ramona's questions were vague, probing, and deflected the moment Patricia tried to press for specifics, instead asking questions herself that were both vague, probing. By the time the call disconnected abruptly, Patricia's heart was pounding, a mix of anger and unease swirling in her chest.

She stared at her phone, her mind racing. A setup. A clumsy one, but a setup nonetheless. Gryoti was fishing, desperate to know how much she had uncovered.

When Simon returned from the garage, she met him in the dining room, a mug of coffee in hand. He took it with a quiet "Thanks."

"How'd it go out there?" she asked.

Simon sipped the coffee, seemingly immune to the scalding heat. "I remember installing that system," he said. "It's old school effective, but easily defeated by anyone who knows what they're doing. The new stuff I've ordered will make this place a fortress."

"What's the new stuff?"

"Smart fencing," Simon explained, his tone lightening just a fraction as he warmed to the topic. "It uses vibration, acoustic, and thermal sensors to detect breaches. The Pan-Tilt-Zoom cameras will automatically track intruders. And I've got a non-lethal deterrent system ordered that'll deploy irritant spray."

"Tear gas?" Patricia asked, her brow furrowing.

"No," Simon said with a slight shake of his head. "PAVA spray. Stronger, longer lasting than conventional pepper spray. We'll use automated nozzles to direct it precisely where it's needed."

"What about animals? We have feral cats."

"The controller uses AI to tell the difference between humans and animals," Simon said with confidence.

"What about drones? They used a drone to deliver the note."

"I can add a drone defeat system."

She nodded. "Are all these technologies reliable?"

Simon's crooked smile returned, and for a moment, the weight of the day lifted. "It's all been used by the military for years. Trust me, Patricia, no one's getting past this system."

Patricia allowed herself to relax, even if just a little. "I can't wait to see it in action."

Simon's caramel eyes held hers for a moment, steady and unwavering. "You'll be safe."

And for the first time since the investigation began, she believed it.

CHAPTER 23

That afternoon, Patricia sat cross-legged on the family room couch, her laptop balanced precariously on a pillow, and a cold cup of coffee sitting untouched on the side table. She scrolled through Instagram, Facebook, and X, her eyes narrowing as she keyed in the search term: Magnum Oncology complaints. Posts began to populate the screen—angry paragraphs, tearful stories, and even a few blurry photos of malpractice claims.

Her stomach churned as she clicked through one after another, jotting notes into a spiral notebook. "Disgruntled patients," she murmured to herself. "Disgruntled and scared."

She was surprised when most of the posters she contacted were eager to talk. Over the phone, one by one, they shared their pain: missed diagnoses, botched treatments, and most disturbingly, a name that kept surfacing—Judy. The same name as the woman who had killed her mother and fled.

"She called me three times," one woman told Patricia, her voice hoarse with exhaustion. "Practically begged me to sign their stupid NDA. Told me it was 'for my own good.' When I refused, I started getting letters in the mail, weird phone calls at night."

"Did you keep any of those letters?" Patricia asked, gripping her pen tighter.

"No. I was too scared. I burned them."

Patricia sighed. "I understand," she said gently, though inside frustration clawed at her. "And Gryoti, did you ever meet with him directly?"

"Yes, and he's a monster. A smug, arrogant monster."

Each conversation was a weight pressing heavier on Patricia's shoulders. Hour after hour, she dialed numbers, scribbling key fragments of stories in her notebook. The accounts were chillingly similar—patients left sicker than before, families devastated, lives ruined. By late afternoon, her fingers trembled as she reached for another number.

"Hello?" The voice on the other end was rough and hesitant.

"Hi, my name is Patricia," she began, her tone as soft as she could manage. "I'm investigating malpractice claims against Magnum Oncology. I saw your post online and was wondering if you'd be willing to share your experience."

There was a long pause, followed by a heavy sigh. "I don't know what good it'll do."

"It matters," Patricia said firmly. "Every story matters. Please, anything you can tell me."

The woman hesitated before speaking. "There's someone you should talk to. Skylar Clear. She used to work for Magnum but quit because of all the fraud going on. If anyone knows something useful, it's her."

Patricia sat up straighter. "Do you know how I can reach her?"

"I'll send you her number. But be careful. These people don't play around."

Patricia exhaled, a mix of relief and determination coursing through her. "Thank you."

The call completed, Patricia sat at the desk, notebook splayed open in front of her. The late-afternoon sunlight poured through the window, casting slivers of light across the page, where names, dates, and fragmented stories crowded the margins in her hurried handwriting. She stared at the words, feeling their weight settle on her shoulders. Each one represented a life that had been diminished, distorted, or outright destroyed by Gryoti's manipulations.

Lucius Alton's care had been her starting point. His story —the misplaced trust, the never-ending treatments, and the continued spread of his cancer—had spurred her on. But now, Lucius wasn't the only face she saw when she closed her eyes.

She sipped her coffee, bitter and cold, and flipped back through the pages of her notebook. Abigail Tran, a promising violinist fighting for her life after a failed experimental procedure Gryoti had sworn would "revolutionize the field." Marcus Heller, a father of three who could no longer recognize his own children after being subjected to a drug trial without full disclosure. Eleanor Pines, who whispered to Patricia that she could still hear Gryoti's voice in her head, urging her to sign consent forms she didn't understand.

One story bled into the next, and Patricia realized there was a pattern; a systematic abuse of trust, an exploitation of vulnerability.

Her pen hovered over the notebook, and she drew a line under Lucius's name. He was a genius, but it wasn't just about Lucius anymore. Her jaw tightened, and she wrote in bold, decisive strokes: *For all of them.*

It was a simple phrase, but it resounded in her chest like the low rumble of a distant storm. She underlined the words twice.

She would need to revisit Gryoti's files, dig deeper into the records, and get every detail she could. This was bigger than her friend. This was about every life that man had touched and twisted. Lucius had given her the spark to start this fight. The others had turned it into an inferno. Justice wasn't a personal quest anymore. It was a duty.

Patricia made a silent vow. No matter what it cost her she would see this through. Gryoti would answer for what he had done.

Patricia picked up her phone, called Skylar, and arranged to meet her for breakfast the next day.

THE FOLLOWING MORNING, THE AIR IN MIRABELLE CAFE WAS filled with the aroma of freshly brewed coffee and the faint sweetness of the bakery counter. Patricia was seated at a corner table, her eyes scanning the room with practiced ease. No threats. She wore a crisp khaki shirtdress that accentuated her lean frame, her hair loosely styled as if she hadn't tried too hard—though she always did. A delicate pearl necklace rested just above her collarbone, adding a touch of simple elegance.

When Skylar Clear stepped inside, Patricia knew instantly it was her. Skylar's auburn braid and hazel eyes gave her an understated yet striking presence. Dressed in a light-gray blouse and tailored black slacks, Skylar moved with the confidence of someone who preferred to go unnoticed and, like Patricia, always knew the exits. She hesitated briefly, her sharp gaze sweeping the room until her eyes met Patricia's.

"Skylar?" Patricia asked, rising slightly and extending her hand.

"Yes," Skylar said, her voice edged with curiosity. She shook Patricia's hand firmly, her grip as steady as her gaze.

"Patricia Falcon. It's nice to meet you. Please, have a seat."

Skylar slid into the chair opposite Patricia, placing a leather-bound notebook on the table before glancing at the menu.

"I hope you don't mind—I ordered us both the peach cobbler waffles," Patricia said with a warm smile. "I hear they're the best in Savannah."

Skylar's lips curved into a small, reluctant smile. "No complaints here."

The server arrived moments later, placing the waffles before them. Patricia's macadamia nut latte and Skylar's lavender chai followed, filling the table with an enticing blend of scents.

They ate in companionable silence for the first few minutes, then exchanged pleasantries about the charm of Savannah, the weather, and their mutual love of the café's cozy atmosphere.

But soon, the light conversation shifted.

"So, Skylar," Patricia began, her voice soft yet probing, "what made you decide to talk with me?"

Skylar leaned back slightly, her fingers toying with the handle of her teacup. "Because someone needs to know the truth, and no one else seems to be willing to do anything about it. Magnum Oncology is not what it seems."

Patricia's eyes narrowed, as her interest sharpened. "I suspected as much. Tell me about Gryoti."

Skylar took a steadying breath, her expression darkening. "He's not just unethical, he's a predator. He takes advantage of people when they're at their most desperate. For existing patients, he prescribes drugs that are ineffective—placebos, basically. When those fail, and they always do, he convinces them to try his experimental treatments that aren't FDA-approved and aren't covered by insurance. These treatments cost a fortune, Patricia. Families drain their savings. Some take out second mortgages. Gryoti lets them bleed financially until the money's gone—or close to it—and then, only then, he finally prescribes the treatment he should've used in the first place."

Patricia's fork hovered mid-air as the weight of Skylar's words sank in. "And when the real treatment works, Gryoti takes the credit."

Skylar nodded, her jaw tightening. "Exactly. Suddenly, he's the hero. The miracle worker. But it's all a scam. And the worst part is, not everyone survives long enough to get the right treatment."

Patricia set her fork down, her appetite vanished. "Do you have proof?"

Skylar reached for her notebook, flipping it open to reveal a neatly organized folder tucked inside. She slid it across the table.

"These are copies of emails between Gryoti and his patients. You'll see the pattern—his promises, the timing of his drug recommendations, and the payments. It's all there."

Patricia opened the folder and scanned the first few pages. Her eyes widened. "This is exactly what I needed. Skylar, this could be the key to bringing him down."

Skylar offered a faint smile, though her eyes remained shadowed. "You're welcome to it. And you should know, I'm not the only one who's seen what he's doing. Others have left Magnum for the same reasons I did."

Patricia looked up sharply. "Others?"

Skylar nodded. "A nurse, a billing specialist, even one of the lab techs. They all left quietly, but I can put you in touch with them. They might be willing to talk."

Patricia closed the folder, her resolve hardening. "Skylar, this is a turning point. Gryoti won't see this coming."

Skylar's gaze met hers, steady and unflinching. "Just be

careful. He's ruthless, and he's got money to burn. He won't go down without a fight."

Patricia lifted her latte, a smirk tugging at her lips. "I've fought tougher battles. And I've never lost one."

Skylar's smile finally broke through, small but genuine. "Then I think he's in trouble."

The two women finished their breakfast, a quiet understanding settling between them. Patricia paid the bill and tucked the incriminating emails into her leather tote next to her gun, already planning her next steps. As they parted outside Mirabelle, the oak-lined streets of Savannah seemed to shimmer with the promise of justice.

The case was building, though she had no specific evidence the drugs Gryoti was using on Lucius were ineffective, other than the FDA finding on Blanscan. But she had no direct proof Gryoti had actually given Blanscan to Lucius.

Patricia stepped into Beau's modest office at Palmetto Printing. The sharp scent of ink and paper filled the air, mingling with a faint metallic tang. Beau was seated at the small, circular conference table that dominated the room, a space so unassuming it seemed a poor match for a man of his stature. The table's surface was scratched and scuffed, a relic of better days, just like the steel desk against the wall and the faded posters of past printing campaigns.

Beau rose as she entered. His blue button-down shirt stretched across his broad chest, and his khakis, while simple, were immaculately pressed. Despite his towering size, Beau moved with an elegance that belied his physical presence—a marathon runner's grace mingled with a gentleman's poise.

"Patricia," he greeted, his deep voice carrying a warmth that instantly set her at ease. His handshake was firm but careful. "Come on in."

She slid into one of the two chairs opposite him, the worn leather creaking slightly under her. The harsh fluorescent light overhead flickered for a moment, casting shadows across Beau's symmetrical face. Despite his composure, the lines near his eyes betrayed a lingering weariness, a reminder of the year he had spent behind bars. He carried it well, but there was no mistaking the burden he bore.

"How have you been, Beau?" she asked.

He nodded slowly, his eyes meeting hers. "Good enough," he said, though his tone hinted at something deeper. "I miss practicing medicine."

Patricia leaned forward, elbows resting lightly on the table's edge. "Any news on getting your license back?"

A smile tugged at the corner of his lips, though it didn't reach his eyes. "We're making progress. I'm optimistic. But it's going to take time."

She nodded, understanding the weight of his words. "We may have located Judy," she offered.

Beau's expression sharpened. "Where?"

"Here."

"Is she in custody?" His tone was measured, but the tension in his broad shoulders betrayed his anticipation.

"We're still not certain it's her," Patricia admitted, the words feeling heavier than she expected.

"How'd you find her?"

"Accidentally. We think she could be posing as a lawyer."

"Is she okay?" he asked.

"Apparently, if it's really her."

"When will you know?"

"Soon."

A flicker of something unreadable crossed Beau's face. "You'll keep me updated?"

"Of course."

His demeanor softened. "I've spoken to all the local oncologists I know about Gryoti," he said, leaning back slightly in his chair. "They all have reservations about him and his approach but acknowledge he's had some surprisingly successful cases with his novel treatments." He paused, folding his large hands on the table, his manicured nails gleaming faintly under the fluorescent light. "Gryoti is known for his aggressive approach—high doses of experimental drugs at high frequency. He calls it The Swiss Protocol. They believe he's a fraud, but he's clever, always evading detection." Beau's voice dropped slightly, tinged with frustration. "Fearing reprisals, none are willing to talk with you."

Patricia sighed, feeling the mounting weight of the obstacles she'd faced in the investigation. "I can't blame them." She began briefing him on her findings about Gryoti, the words flowing steadily as she outlined her discoveries.

Beau listened intently, his dark eyes never leaving hers. "Have you considered sending Gryoti a new patient to entrap him into making fraudulent claims and maybe even to obtain samples?" he suggested. "I have a friend with stage-four prostate cancer. He'd be ideal."

Patricia's mind raced. "Great idea, Beau. But I think Lucius might be a better choice. He's already a current patient, and a lawyer. I'll check with him, and if he doesn't agree, we'll use your friend."

Beau nodded approvingly. "Excellent."

CHAPTER 25

Shortly after Trey left for work the following day, Ellery called Patricia and asked to come over. The urgency in her voice was unmistakable, and Patricia agreed without hesitation. A half hour later, Ellery arrived, her face set in grim determination.

Patricia led her to the family room at the back of the house, a warm, inviting space with plush furnishings and bookshelves lined with a century of book collecting by Trey's family. As Ellery took a seat in one of the overstuffed chairs arranged in a conversational cluster before the black marble fireplace, Patricia observed the tension in her posture.

"Would you care for something to drink?" Patricia asked, moving toward the kitchen area adjacent to the family room.

Ellery shook her head, her expression tight. "I'm fine."

Patricia sat across from her, carefully watching Ellery's face. They exchanged pleasantries for a moment, but it was clear Ellery had something pressing to say.

"I received a threatening note." She retrieved a folded piece of paper from her purse and handed it to Patricia. "I'm guessing it came from Gryoti."

Patricia unfolded the note and read the stark, hand-written message: *Stop investigating or you'll lose your pension.*

Patricia frowned and met Ellery's eyes. "When did you get this?"

"It was on my doorstep this morning," Ellery replied. Her voice wavered slightly, but she quickly composed herself. Without another word, she reached into her purse again and produced a photograph, passing it to Patricia. It was a picture of a bedroom.

Patricia stiffened. "They were in your house?"

Ellery nodded, her jaw clenched. "In my bedroom. They know where I sleep."

A chill ran through Patricia. "Give me a moment." She opened the photo app on her phone, scrolled to the photo she'd taken of the first note, and held it next to the second note.

"Same handwriting. Same calculated tone. This isn't just intimidation, they're escalating. Do you have security video?"

Ellery sighed. "No. I never thought I'd need it."

"Have you discussed my investigation with anyone?"

Ellery shook her head. "No one, outside of you."

Patricia leaned back, thinking. "Then how would Gryoti know you were involved?"

"He may have someone following you. He may even be tracking your phone calls. Somehow, he's linked us." She took a deep breath, then exhaled slowly. "My pension ... Who does he know that can mess with my retirement benefits?"

"I'm so sorry, Ellery," Patricia said, her tone heavy with concern.

"I'm mad," Ellery snapped, gripping the armrests of the chair. "And I'm not giving in to him. Any help you need from me, you've got it."

Patricia nodded. "I appreciate that."

Ellery's eyes burned with determination. "The work you're doing is important. And it's personal to me. My grandmother was duped by false cancer treatments."

Patricia's heart clenched at the revelation. She reached out and gave Ellery's hand a squeeze.

Ellery lifted the note again and studied it. "An innocent man doesn't send threatening notes. These are an admission of guilt."

"But we can't convict him for sending two notes," Patricia pointed out.

Ellery nodded. "You need to get someone on the inside."

"I have a plan. I'm going to try to recruit my friend Lucius to help. He's a current patient, and a lawyer. If I can get him to record his conversations with Gryoti, we might get enough evidence to expose what's really going on."

Ellery considered this for a moment. "Georgia is a one-party consent state, so there's no problem there. Also have him do everything possible to get a sample of what they're giving him."

Patricia nodded. The conversation shifted to rules of evidence and the importance of securing a clear chain of custody for anything Patricia gathered.

After Ellery left, Patricia filed the second note and photo, then returned to calling former employees of Magnum. Each one had the same story—grand promises of miraculous treatments but no results. Most of what they said corroborated what she already knew. Then, a former Magnum bookkeeper mentioned something new: Gryoti had ties to a corrupt official on the Georgia Composite Medical Board.

"In exchange for huge bribes, this official has been turning a blind eye to Gryoti's illegal activities," the bookkeeper confided.

Patricia's pulse quickened. "Do you have a name?"

She jotted down the name the bookkeeper gave her and wasted no time in asking Meredith to dig into any documentation that could prove bribes had taken place.

LATER THAT AFTERNOON, PATRICIA MET WITH ISABEL AT HER home. In a quiet sitting room, she briefed her friend on the progress of the investigation, including her plan to bring Lucius in as an informant. Isabel listened carefully, then nodded. "Let's talk to him."

They met Lucius in his den, a stately room lined with law books and framed certificates. The elderly lawyer looked weary but alert.

"How have you been, Lucius?" Patricia asked.

"Up and down," he admitted. "Mostly up today."

"At my request," Isabel said. "Patricia looked into one of your cancer drugs."

Lucius's eyes widened. "Why?"

"I was curious why it didn't work," Isabel said carefully. She turned to Patricia. "What did you find?"

"One of the drugs Magnum gave you is on an FDA list of fake drugs."

Lucius blinked. "Are you sure?"

Patricia nodded. "I double-checked."

"I saw the citation myself, Dad," Isabel added. "Magnum infused you with a fake drug called Blanscan."

Lucius's expression darkened. "And an outrageously expensive one at that." He exhaled sharply.

"There's more, Lucius," Patricia said, leaning forward.

With his full attention, she laid out everything she had discovered.

Lucius looked between them, then at the floor. "Why didn't you tell me about Patricia's investigation earlier?" he asked Isabel.

"There was no point in alarming you if everything turned out to be legitimate."

"But it wasn't," he said grimly. "What's the next step?"

Patricia detailed the plan to entrap Gryoti and obtain a sample of the drug.

Lucius straightened. "I'm game. Let's bring him down."

CHAPTER 26

The following morning, sunlight poured through the large window in the kitchen, casting a soft glow across the glass table and wide-plank oak floors. The uneven plaster walls, tinged with a faint peach hue, seemed to shimmer in the morning light. Beyond the window, the backyard lay still.

Patricia poured a glass mug of coffee and glanced at Trey. Dressed in a worn, brown-tweed blazer over a plain white T-shirt and faded jeans, he exuded an effortless confidence.

"You're not reading the paper," Patricia said, her voice light but her gaze sharp as she blew on her coffee.

Trey looked up, his deep-set brown eyes shadowed, and rubbed his jawline, where stubble emphasized the strength of his Roman nose and tapered cheeks. "I don't want to alarm you, Patsy, but we had another break-in last night," he said, his Southern drawl stretching the words like molasses, calm and unhurried despite the weight of the revelation.

"What happened?"

"When I got up this morning, I noticed my laptop wasn't plugged into the charger and was in a slightly different place than where I normally put it. You know what a creature of habit I am."

She nodded, gripping her mug as though it were a lifeline, her face maintaining a mask of calm while her mind raced. The faint sound of the grandfather clock ticking in the foyer filled the silence.

"Suspecting the worst, I checked our security video," Trey continued. "Around two this morning, someone used our passcode to enter the front door. They went directly to your office, opened your laptop, and tried to boot it up. Failing that, they went to the family room and tried, unsuccessfully, to boot my computer up. They had our door entry code, Patsy, and moved through the house as though they knew exactly where our laptops were. They left after a few minutes without disturbing anything else."

"Any idea who?"

Trey shook his head, leaning back in the chair, which creaked faintly under his weight. "No. They were masked."

"Gryoti's doing?"

"Has to be," he said without hesitation.

Patricia's gaze flickered to the backyard and then to the back door, her thoughts darting to the safety of their home. The backyard outside the window was peaceful, but the weight of her investigation hung heavy in the air. The notes. The email. The vandalism to her car. The break-ins. All warnings, plain as day, from Gryoti. No time for bravado when a murderer was after them.

"Ellery's home a couple of nights ago, and now ours. A second time at that. We need to get Simon more involved. We need him here full-time," she said.

Trey nodded, his expression darkening as he rubbed his temple, the cowlick in his chestnut hair catching the morning light. "Yeah. Full-court press. No stone unturned.

We can't afford to take any more chances. I'll call him now." Trey reached for his phone.

Patricia tightened her grip on the mug, drawing strength from Trey's unshakable presence, even as unease settled deep in her chest. "And Hayley—she's too exposed at college, Trey. She needs protection too."

"I'll get full-time security for her, don't worry."

Patricia sighed, her fingers tracing the edge of her mug. "And Trey?"

"Yes, darlin'?"

"Don't forget about yourself. Gryoti's a killer. You never know who he might target."

"He'll have a hard time getting to me. And if he tries, I guarantee he'll regret it," Trey said, his voice like granite.

Her eyes met his. "I love you."

"Love you too," he said.

CHAPTER 27

Shortly after Trey left for work, Simon called to let Patricia know he'd be right over. No sooner than she'd put her phone down, it came to life again.

She didn't recognize the number, but instinct told her to answer.

"Patricia Falcon speaking."

A brief pause, then a woman's voice, touched with a Savannah drawl, said, "Ms. Falcon, my name is Margaret Delacroix. People call me Maggie. I believe you spoke with my friend Celeste Wright about Magnum Oncology."

Patricia straightened in her chair. Celeste had hinted at others who might be willing to talk, but so far, no one else had called.

"Yes," Patricia said, careful to keep her voice neutral. "Celeste mentioned someone. She said you might have information."

A long exhale crackled through the line. When Maggie spoke again, her voice was wary. "I do. And it's important. But I'd rather not talk over the phone."

Patricia understood Maggie's hesitation. If the woman

had something solid, something dangerous, she wouldn't want to risk being overheard, or traced.

"I get it," Patricia said. "Where would you feel comfortable meeting?"

"My house," Maggie answered immediately. "I know how that sounds, but I'd rather talk where I feel safe. You understand?"

Patricia did. People handled risks in different ways. Some met in public, hoping to blend into the crowd. Others needed the comfort of their own space to find the courage to speak at all.

"I do understand," Patricia assured her. "Does this afternoon work for you?"

"Yes," Maggie said, relief slipping into her voice. "Two o'clock?"

"I'll be there."

Maggie gave her an address in Savannah's historic district. Patricia jotted it down on the notepad she kept beside the phone, her handwriting precise.

As she set the phone down, she let out a breath she hadn't realized she was holding. A gust of wind rattled the mullioned door leading to the backyard. Patricia glanced toward it, feeling the weight of what she'd just agreed to.

Maggie Delacroix had just taken the first step. Now, Patricia had to find out if the woman was handing her a key to the case or painting a target on both of their backs.

Patricia dumped the half-pot of coffee Trey had made much earlier and made a fresh pot of Black Rifle Coffee, Simon's favorite. She took a moment to savor the bold aroma as it filled the kitchen, a small comfort amid the uncertainty that loomed over her investigation.

She was reading emails at the kitchen table when her phone rang again. She glanced at the screen and accepted the call.

"Hello, Willie. How ya doing?" she asked.

"It's a lovely day in Savannah," he said. "How are you?"

"This business with Gryoti is heating up. The more I discover about him, the more he threatens us. We had a break-in last night that was probably his doing. And he's threatening the people who talk with me. I've never seen anything like it. But enough of me, how are you doing with Gryoti on the book?"

"That's why I called. Gryoti has broken off all communication with me. No excuse given."

"Well, getting him to open up to you was a long shot. At least he hasn't resorted to threatening you."

The front door chimes went off.

"Do you have anything else, Willie?" Patricia stood and headed toward the front of the house.

"No. That's it. Stay safe, Patricia."

"You too."

Patricia shoved the phone in her back pocket and checked the video monitor in the foyer. Simon. She opened the door.

"That didn't take long. Come in. I just made a fresh pot of coffee. Care for a cup?"

Simon, dressed in a black T-shirt and black tactical pants, picked up his two duffels and stepped in. "I'd love a mug," he said, heading down the hall to the dining room.

Patricia went to the kitchen, poured coffee, and returned to the dining room. Simon had already unzipped one of his duffels, spreading out a sleek laptop, several compact surveillance devices, and a handful of other gear that looked straight out of a spy thriller.

Simon took the mug. "I heard you had a break-in."

"Last night. Front door. They had our passcode."

"I'll get on that first." He took a long drink, put the mug down on the table, and headed back to the front door. "I'll let you know if I find anything."

Patricia had just settled down at her desk when Simon came into her office. He held up two small black cubes.

"What are those?" she asked.

"Battery-operated micro video transponders. They were placed in the shrubs on either side of your door with a clear line of sight to your digital keypad."

"Now what?"

"They're offline now. I'll change your passcode, then I'll order retina identification devices for both doors. I don't know when they'll come in, but I'll put a rush on it."

"Thank you, Simon."

He smiled and gestured toward the dining room. "I'm going to check the security video to see if I can pinpoint when these transponders were placed."

Patricia nodded and turned back to her desk, her mind already shifting to the next move in the investigation. The pieces were beginning to fall into place, but so were the dangers.

With her meeting with Maggie Delacroix looming, she had the distinct feeling she was stepping into the lion's den.

Around one thirty, Patricia let Simon know she was going out to interview a whistleblower.

"Do you know her?"

"No."

"Did you run a background check?"

"I checked her social media. She seems to have been in Savannah for some time."

"Do you want me to come with you?" Simon asked, glancing up from the security feed on his laptop.

"No. I think she'll speak more freely one-on-one."

Simon frowned but nodded. "Okay. I'll sweep the house for bugs while you're gone."

Patricia hesitated near the door. "Did the security video show who placed the transponders?"

"They knew what they were doing. Fully masked. Whoever it was, they weren't amateurs."

Patricia exhaled. "Of course they weren't."

She slipped on a black leather jacket and headed to the back door, her boots clicking on the floor. The air outside carried the crisp bite of fall.

Just before two, Patricia climbed the stairs to Maggie's wraparound porch. The house loomed before her, a relic from a time when craftsmanship meant something. Its white paint was peeling in spots, and the iron railings had flecks of rust, but the structure itself stood strong. The scent of damp wood mixed with the faint tang of old brick, giving the air a heavy, almost historical weight.

Patricia rang the doorbell and deep chimes echoed inside. She adjusted her stance, listening. Footsteps approached, then the massive double doors creaked open.

Patricia's breath caught. Judy.

A gun was gripped in her left hand, her knuckles white around the polished black metal. The sight of the weapon was jarring, but it was Judy's choice of hand that sent an alarm ringing through Patricia's mind. Judy was right-handed. If she was using her left hand that meant any restoration of her right hand had been for appearance only.

"Come in. Or if you wish, I can just shoot you here and drag your body in," Judy said, her voice cool and edged with venom.

Patricia met her gaze, refusing to flinch. "Hello, Judy." She kept her hands at her sides, steadying her breath. If she made one wrong move, she wouldn't leave this house alive.

Patricia stepped left after entering to allow the sun glare

to constrict Judy's pupils and to permit her own to adjust to the much dimmer light of the foyer.

The air was thick with the scent of old wood and dust, a stark contrast to the grandeur the home must have once displayed. Faded velvet furniture sat beneath heavy drapes that blocked the daylight. Shadows stretched unnaturally in the dim lighting.

Patricia's sharp eyes scanned for movement. No reinforcements. Judy was alone, though that didn't make her less dangerous.

"Put your purse with that gun of yours on the floor," Judy ordered, tilting the barrel slightly for emphasis.

Patricia hesitated, calculating. Every second mattered.

"Now," Judy directed, "or I'll take your right hand like you took mine."

Slowly, Patricia knelt, placing her purse on the marble floor. She edged it aside with her foot, shifting her weight subtly. The moment had to be perfect.

"Raise your hands," Judy snapped.

Patricia complied, lifting them chest high in the ready position she'd drilled into her muscle memory during self-defense training. Her pulse pounded, but her mind was razor-sharp. *Get your head straight, Patricia. You only have one chance to take that gun. Focus.*

"I should have known you'd try something like this," Patricia said, keeping Judy engaged.

Judy smirked. "You always did think you were smarter than me. How's that working out for you?"

Patricia inhaled sharply, then her arms shot out, locking both hands around the gun with a vicelike grip. At the same instant, she dropped into a squat, pulling Judy off balance. The gun discharged, the sharp pop deafening in the enclosed space. The bullet embedded into the wainscoting, inches from Patricia's shoulder.

Ignoring the acrid scent of gunpowder, Patricia shifted her weight, stepping forward with her right foot. She twisted her body left, wrenching Judy's arm forward. Judy stumbled, her wrist contorting at an unnatural angle. Patricia capitalized on the moment, wrapping her right arm over Judy's left, securing the weapon between them.

Another shot fired, lodging into the far wall.

Patricia stomped down hard on Judy's foot. The crack of bone wasn't loud, but Judy's howl of pain was. With all the power she could muster, Patricia twisted Judy's wrist back toward her forearm with precision, leveraging her body weight against the tendons.

When the wrist snapped, Judy screamed, her fingers spasming open. The gun clattered to the floor.

In one swift motion, Patricia snatched it up and stepped back beyond Judy's reach. She leveled the weapon at Judy's center mass, steady and unshaking.

Judy panted, chest rising and falling with fury. Patricia saw the calculation in her gaze, the slow realization that she had lost.

"You try anything stupid, and you'll lose your left hand," Patricia warned. "You know I can do it."

Judy's nostrils flared, but she held still. "This isn't over, Patricia."

Patricia exhaled slowly, keeping the gun trained. "Oh, I think it is." She reached into her pocket and pulled out her phone. "Now, let's call the police, shall we?"

CHAPTER 28

When Patricia returned home after Judy's apprehension, she wasted no time. She strode through the kitchen, the echo of her boots tapping against the polished hardwood floors.

She found Simon in the dining room sitting at the expansive cherrywood table, his laptop open in front of him. A cup of coffee sat forgotten at his side, the steam long since dissipated. His expression was tense, his fingers tapping absently on the wood as he scrolled through pages of information. He looked up as Patricia entered, instantly recognizing the urgency in her gaze.

"We got her," Patricia announced without preamble, her voice sharp with both satisfaction and frustration. "Judy's in custody."

"That's a step forward, but not the finish line."

"Exactly. With Judy's arrest, we've struck a blow to Gryoti's operation, but we still don't have enough evidence to convict him of the crimes he's engaged in." She hesitated to settle her mind. "Lucius Alton has agreed to wear a wire at his appointment this afternoon. He's stopping by here first so you can set him up."

"Does he have a smartphone?"

"Yes," Patricia confirmed, taking a seat across from him.

"Then we'll use that," Simon said. He closed his laptop and reached for a small device in his bag, setting it on the table. "I'll show him how. It'll just take a minute or two."

A silence settled between them, the weight of their mission pressing heavily. The dining room, with its rich mahogany paneling and gilded mirror reflecting the chandelier lights, had hosted many conversations over the years—some filled with laughter, others with secrets. Today, it would bear witness to yet another piece of the unfolding puzzle.

Around three thirty, Isabel and Lucius arrived. The moment they stepped inside, Patricia could see the nervous tension in Lucius's posture. His fingers twitched slightly, jaw tight. Isabel, ever the steadying force, gave him a reassuring pat on the back.

"Let's get started," Simon said, motioning them toward the dining table.

Lucius sat down, shifting uncomfortably as Simon took his phone and installed the recording app. "You just need to keep your phone in your pocket," Simon explained. "It'll pick up everything within a few feet, so as long as Gryoti isn't whispering, we'll have solid audio."

"And if he catches on?" Lucius asked.

"He won't," Patricia assured him. "Just act normal. You're there for a consultation about the next steps, nothing else. Keep the conversation flowing naturally."

Lucius nodded, though his eyes flickered with uncertainty.

"You're doing the right thing," Isabel whispered, squeezing his shoulder.

After running through a quick test, Simon played back the sample recording. The audio was crisp and clear. Satisfied, he handed Lucius's phone back to him.

"You're set," Simon said. "Go do what you need to do. We'll be here waiting."

Lucius and Isabel returned just after five, the tension in their expressions making Patricia's pulse quicken. They walked straight to the dining table, Lucius pulling out his phone with slightly unsteady hands.

"It worked," he said.

Patricia didn't hesitate. "Let's hear it."

Simon connected the phone to his laptop, and moments later, Gryoti's voice filled the dining room, smooth and controlled, yet undeniably sinister.

GRYOTI: How are you feeling today?

LUCIUS: Unhappy the last treatment didn't work and curious about where we go from here.

GRYOTI: We have excellent CT scans of your tumors, and while they're still present, the good news is they haven't grown. But slowing or halting growth is not our objective. We want to eliminate your cancer, so now we go on to the next level of chemo.

LUCIUS: Is this bad?

GRYOTI: I don't want you to be concerned. Different cancers react differently to our products. We keep trying until something works.

LUCIUS: What if nothing works?

GRYOTI: We have many alternatives.

LUCIUS: What will the next chemo be?

GRYOTI: I haven't decided yet, but rest assured, whatever I choose will be the best one for your situation.

LUCIUS: You seem optimistic about eliminating my cancer.

GRYOTI: Absolutely. My products work. Try not to worry. We do this every day. Any other concerns?

LUCIUS: No. Thank you, Doctor.

GRYOTI: We'll see you tomorrow for your next infusion.

THE ROOM WAS DEATHLY SILENT WHEN THE RECORDING ENDED.

Patricia exhaled slowly. "That was cleaner than I expected. Gryoti didn't just hint at his treatments, he openly claimed his products work."

Simon nodded. "And with his history, this could be enough to begin to build a case against him. We're close."

Patricia turned to Lucius. "Are you ready for tomorrow's infusion?"

Lucius hesitated only a second before nodding. "My part's easy—I just have to sit in the chair. Are you ready?"

"I sure am," Patricia said, a determined smile tugging at her lips. "With any luck, by this time tomorrow, we'll have the sample we need to convict Gryoti."

The weight of their mission settled over them like a tangible force, but for the first time in days, Patricia felt something close to hope.

Tomorrow, they would take the next step. And this time, they wouldn't just be gathering evidence.

They would be setting the final trap.

CHAPTER 29

"This is it." Patricia turned to Lucius, who sat in the passenger seat of the Navigator. "Are you ready?"

Despite his age and stage-four cancer, his eyes were alert and piercing, like an eagle on the hunt. "Absolutely."

As soon as oncoming traffic passed, Patricia turned off the main road at the discreet Magnum Oncology sign, the chrome letters catching the morning sunlight in a dazzling glint. A smooth asphalt road led into a grove of old oak trees. They emerged from the grove to a distant office building set amid an immense manicured lawn.

She closed the distance to the single-story Magnum building, a masterful blend of modern efficiency and compassionate design—or at least, the illusion of it. The clean lines of steel and pale gray stone gave it the imposing gravitas of a research institute, but the vast, reflective windows softened the effect, catching the morning light and throwing it back in a golden haze. It was almost too perfect; the kind of beauty meant to pacify patients and reassure families. Hope carefully engineered.

Patricia parked not far from the building. Security cameras hung from the corners. As she and Lucius approached the entrance, the automatic glass doors whooshed open with a whisper, ushering them into the softly lit reception area.

The sterile scent of antiseptic filled her nose, its sharpness cut by a faint trace of lavender—pumped through the vents, she guessed, to settle the nerves of those who feared what awaited beyond these walls. The soft hum of the ventilation system was a constant backdrop, an ever-present reminder of air carefully filtered, controlled, and monitored. Security cameras were strategically placed to cover every inch of the lobby.

The walls were painted in calming shades of cool blue and muted green, broken up by abstract art—swirling over-sized canvases of color that offered no focus, no sense of grounding. A deliberate choice, she thought. Something to absorb the mind, to distract.

They bypassed the carefully spaced chairs, each occupied by solitary figures lost in smartphone screens, and approached the black marble reception counter. The woman behind the desk, in crisp medical scrubs, greeted them with a bright, well-practiced smile.

"Hello, Mr. Alton," she chirped, her voice hitting that perfect note of professional warmth. "So good to see you again. You didn't bring your daughter, Isabel, today?" Her gaze flicked briefly to Patricia, her expression polite but subtly assessing.

"Isabel is busy," Lucius said, returning the receptionist's smile with one of his own. "This is Mrs. Falcon, a close friend who offered to keep me company during treatment." His frail hand brushed Patricia's arm briefly—a fleeting gesture, meant to affirm her presence.

"Hello, Mrs. Falcon." The receptionist's lips stretched a little wider, but her eyes didn't quite warm. She slid a sleek tablet across the counter. "Would you mind signing in? Just for our records."

"Not at all." Patricia picked up the device, the cool glass smooth against her fingertips. She entered her full name and handed the tablet back. She wondered if her name would trigger something in Magnum's security system.

Soon after, a nurse in blue scrubs entered the room, her posture upright, efficient, but not unkind. Her nametag read Elizabeth.

"Good morning, Mr. Alton," she greeted warmly, tablet in hand.

"Hello, Elizabeth." Lucius inclined his bald head slightly, then gestured toward Patricia. "This is Patricia. She'll be sitting with me today."

"Pleased to meet you, Patricia." Elizabeth handed them disposable face masks, gesturing for them to put them on before leading them down a long, hushed hallway.

The infusion atrium was a space designed for comfort, or at least the illusion of it. There were no obvious security cameras. Each walled cubicle had a recliner, a guest chair, and a small table. Lucius chose a cubicle at the far end, near a casement window overlooking a meticulously landscaped garden. A strategic choice to remain mostly out of sight of the nurses' station. His gaze met Patricia's for a moment. A silent understanding passed between them.

Patricia took her seat, pulling out her phone and pretending to scroll through emails while Elizabeth worked efficiently, hanging an IV bag and hooking Lucius up. The IV pump beeped softly as she adjusted the settings. Patricia memorized everything—the labeling on the IV bag, the tubing, the settings on the monitor.

After a few final checks, Elizabeth nodded. "Let me know

if you need anything," she said, then exited toward the nurses' station.

After fifteen minutes, Patricia stood, moving toward the window with deliberate casualness. She inhaled slowly, schooling her expression into something thoughtful.

"It's so beautiful outside," she murmured, nodding toward the garden as if lost in admiration.

"Yes, it is," Lucius said softly. The code. The signal that no one was watching.

Patricia's pulse quickened, but her hands remained steady. She stepped closer to the IV pole, positioning herself so that her body shielded her actions from view.

Her fingers slipped into her jacket pocket, closing around a syringe. The cool plastic felt almost foreign against the warmth of her palm, a stark contrast to the light sheen of sweat forming on her skin.

With a quick glance over her shoulder, she removed the needle cover in a single, practiced motion.

Tilting the IV bag up just enough to prevent any telltale leak, she eased the needle into the bag. The soft give of the plastic barely registered as she withdrew ten mL of liquid. She put the bag back in its normal position and slid the needle cover back into place with a click.

Exhaling slowly, she returned the syringe to her pocket, resisting the urge to check if anyone had noticed.

"These clouds are magnificent," she said, turning back to Lucius with a measured smile, signaling completion.

She sank back into her chair, forcing herself to relax, though her mind remained alert. The classical music filtering from the overhead speakers seemed suddenly more pronounced—a gentle wash of sound meant to keep the atmosphere calm, in control.

Slowly, she reached into her pocket and transferred the

syringe into a refrigerated packet provided by Ellery. She checked the seal, ensuring everything was in place.

In three hours, Ellery would stop by Patricia's house to pick up the refrigerated sample and transport it to a local DEA-approved laboratory. With any luck, by the end of the day they'd know exactly what Magnum had been dripping into Lucius.

CHAPTER 30

Around one, Patricia's front door chimed. She pushed away from her desk, went to the foyer, and checked the security video. Ellery Hampton was on time to pick up the sample.

"It's Ellery," shouted to Simon.

Patricia opened the door, greeted Ellery, and led her to the family room as they chatted.

"Would you care for something to drink? Water? Tea?"

"No thank you."

Patricia gestured for Ellery to sit in one of the chairs facing the fireplace, then sat herself.

The midday sunlight casted soft patterns across the Persian carpet. Patricia sat forward on the overstuffed chair, her elbows on her knees, gripping the worn leather notebook where she had meticulously summarized her notes on Gryoti's medical fraud scheme. Across from her, Ellery leaned back in the matching chair that seemed to swallow her small frame.

"I really think we've got enough evidence, Ellery." Patricia's voice was measured but determined. "We have Judy in custody, patient and employee testimonies, the recording of Gryoti making false claims, and the drug sample. Once we get confirmation the sample has no cancer-fighting capability, we should take this to the authorities immediately before Gryoti catches on and runs. Considering how involved Judy was in his operation, he must be concerned that she has been arrested and might cooperate with the authorities."

Ellery crossed one ankle over the other and rubbed her thumb along the edge of her jaw. "You've done impressive work, Patricia. Really. But this case is like a hydra. Cut off one head and another will grow in its place." She sat forward slightly, meeting Patricia's gaze. "Yes, Gryoti's the face of the fraud. But what about the others behind him? The accountants who helped move the money? The nurses who administered the drugs? The people who formulated them? And the politician who took bribes to protect Gryoti? If we hand everything over now, the authorities might only get Gryoti."

Patricia tapped her pen against the notebook. "You're saying we'd be cutting the investigation short."

"Yes. Think of it like this: You've tracked the smoke back to the fire, but you haven't found the fuel or the matches. There's a money trail here. Gryoti didn't squirrel away all that cash without help. If we follow the trail further, we might uncover co-conspirators and locate the money he's stashed away."

Patricia's eyes drifted to the flickering embers in the fireplace. "That makes sense. If we find the money, we give the authorities a stronger case. But how do we know where to go next? Meredith has already combed through his bank records."

"True," Ellery agreed, "but fraud like this rarely sticks to the obvious paths. Offshore accounts, shell companies, even property bought in relatives' names. There's a pattern to follow, and I'd wager it's hidden in the records Meredith found."

Patricia flipped through her notes and found the section marked with a yellow tab. "Like the unusually high payments to Savannah Medical Logistics?"

"Exactly." Ellery's eyes lit with encouragement. "We dig into that. Who owns the company? What kind of business are they in? Who do they bribe? Small steps could lead us to Gryoti's entire financial network."

"Meredith says the bulk of his money is overseas."

"In his name?"

"I believe so."

"Where?"

"A bank in the Bahamas." Patricia consulted her summary. "The Commonwealth Bank."

Ellery scribbled a note. "The DEA has an office in the Bahamas. The current head of the Caribbean Division is an old friend. I'll see if we can get access to the account."

"Thank you."

"And don't forget about domestic assets. Remember the whistleblower telling you Gryoti pays off politicians? Those transactions might have been entirely in the United States. His daughter's education? Probably paid with funds from a US account. That impressive clinic of his was probably built with domestic money."

Patricia let out a long breath and sat back in her chair. "I guess I was just too eager to wrap this up, you know? I wanted to get it off the table."

"And that's understandable," Ellery said. "Most people would've stopped once they found the fraudulent claim. But you're not most people. You're curious, thorough. That's what makes you so good at this."

Patricia smiled, the tension in her shoulders easing.

"Thanks, Ellery. I appreciate your faith in me. And your patience."

Ellery's lips quirked into a half-smile. "Anytime. Now, I'll do my part and take the sample to the lab and make sure it gets analyzed immediately. And I'll check up on Gryoti's Bahamas account."

Patricia set the notebook on the glass-topped coffee table. "I'm glad I didn't go straight to the authorities. You were right. There's much more to uncover."

Ellery gave a nod. "And we'll get there, Patricia. One lead at a time."

After Ellery left, Patricia put on a light jacket and walked to Summer's home. The air was crisp and the sun bright. Summer greeted her at the door. They chatted as Summer led her to the living room.

Patricia sat on the overstuffed couch; her hands wrapped tightly around a mug of tea Summer brought. The soft glow of a vintage floor lamp illuminated the book-shelves packed with psychology texts and novels. Outside, the muffled hum of Savannah's traffic drifted through the lace curtains.

Summer settled into the armchair across from Patricia, her posture relaxed but her eyes focused. She wore a navy-blue shift, her auburn hair piled in its trademark messy bun. The air between them was warm, yet Patricia's tension was palpable.

"Talk to me, darlin'," Summer said, her voice gentle. "What's got you so tied up in knots?"

Patricia exhaled heavily, staring down into her tea. "It's everything, Summer. Trey's been so supportive through all this, but I keep imagining the worst. What if something happens to him? Or Hayley? This investigation has put a target on my back, and I can't help but feel like it's just a matter of time before they get dragged into it too."

Summer leaned forward slightly, her freckled face calm but intent. "It sounds like your mind is running away with all the what-ifs," she said. "And trust me, I get it. But those what-ifs don't help. They only drain your energy and keep you from focusing on what you can control."

"I know that," Patricia said, her voice tight. "But how do I stop? It feels like I'm always on edge, waiting for something to go wrong."

Summer nodded, her fingers tapping lightly on the armrest. "It's natural to feel that way, especially with everything you've been through. But there are ways to take back control. For starters, try structured journaling. Every night, write down your worries and then separate them into two lists: what you can control and what you can't."

Patricia's brow furrowed. "And what does that do?"

"It helps you see things more clearly," Summer explained. "When you put those thoughts on paper, they stop swirling around in your head. And when you focus on the things you can control, you start to feel more empowered."

Patricia took a sip of tea, considering. "That sounds manageable. What else?"

"Mindfulness exercises," Summer said. "When you start feeling overwhelmed, take a moment to ground yourself. Focus on your breath. Count each inhale and exhale. It sounds simple, but it can make a world of difference in calming your mind."

Patricia nodded. "I'll try it. But what about the fear? It's like a constant weight on my chest."

Summer's eyes softened. "Fear is a tricky thing. It's your mind's way of trying to protect you, even when there's no immediate danger. Acknowledge it, but don't let it dictate your actions. When you feel that fear creeping in, remind yourself of the facts. Trey and Hayley are safe, and you're taking every precaution to keep them that way."

Patricia's lips curved into a smile. "I guess that makes sense. It's just hard not to spiral."

"It is," Summer agreed. "But you're not in this alone. You've got a tremendous support system. Lean on us. And don't be afraid to take breaks. Your mind needs rest as much as your body does."

Patricia reached across the small table and squeezed Summer's hand. "Thank you. You always know exactly what to say."

Summer's smile was warm and steady. "That's what I'm here for, darlin'. Now, let's get you set up with that journal. I've got a few extra around here somewhere."

As Summer rose, Patricia felt a small but significant weight lift from her shoulders. The road ahead was still uncertain, but with Summer's guidance, she felt just a little more equipped to face it.

MEREDITH CAME OVER TO PATRICIA'S TO DISCUSS NEXT STEPS.

"Alright, let's go over this again," Patricia said. "We know Gryoti is moving money offshore to the Bahamas, and we have a solid understanding of his credit history and business transactions. We also know he's laundering a lot of money through fake charities and possibly bribing doctors for patient referrals. What's our next step to completely lock down his financial network?"

Meredith tapped her pen against the glass-topped coffee table, her expression thoughtful. "The biggest challenge is finding all his shell accounts and linking them to him definitively. So far, the charities are a clear laundering mechanism, but the real trick is following the money from those charities back to his personal overseas holdings."

"Ellery is checking with her DEA friend in the Caribbean Division to see if she can get access to Gryoti's account at Commonwealth."

"That's good," Meredith said. "The DEA has had a lot of success doing that. If Ellery gets cooperation, we should be able to see all the entities making deposits. In a different vein, I've been using blockchain tracing tools to track Gryoti's cryptocurrency transactions, and there's something suspicious. A series of crypto withdrawals are being converted into cash equivalents—prepaid cards, electronic gift cards, even digital payment platforms that obscure the source."

"So he's not just hiding money offshore," Patricia mused. "He's diversifying through crypto."

"Exactly," Meredith confirmed. "And if we dig deeper, we might find evidence of him using these digital transactions to pay off doctors for referrals. We already suspect the kick-backs, but this could be the proof we need."

Patricia nodded. "Can we subpoena these transactions?"

"Not easily," Meredith admitted. "Crypto transactions are notoriously hard to subpoena unless we find an exchange that complies with regulations. But if I can identify which platform he's using, we might be able to request records under the pretense of investigating medical fraud. It would help if we had law enforcement on our side."

"I'll talk to Algenon at the FBI," Patricia said. "He's been waiting for us to bring him something. If we give him enough, he might be able to pull the right strings to get those records."

"Good. Meanwhile, I'll focus on the shell accounts," Meredith said, reaching into her bag and pulling out a folder. "I did some preliminary digging into the charities Gryoti donates to. A few of them have board members who are nothing more than corporate ghosts—fake identities used to set up the entities. Once Ellery gets access to Gryoti's Commonwealth account, I want to cross-check those charities and ghost names with the offshore account. If any of those entities overlap with Gryoti's known network, we'll have a direct tie."

Patricia leaned back in her chair, absorbing it all. "What about his contributions to politicians?"

"That's another angle we need to explore. Political donations can be a form of influence laundering. If he's funneling money into campaigns, it probably means those politicians are assisting him in some way. We need to see if any legislation has been passed that benefits his clinic or pharmacy."

Patricia rubbed her chin. "Willie could help us there. As an experienced investigative reporter, he could look into the political angle while we focus on the finances."

Meredith smiled. "Sounds good."

Patricia exhaled, her mind racing with the possibilities. "Okay. We divide and conquer. I'll handle Algenon and Willie. You keep drilling down into the charities and shell accounts. If we can tie this all together—offshore accounts, crypto kickbacks, fake charities, and political corruption—we won't just expose Gryoti's fraud, we'll dismantle his entire operation."

Meredith nodded, her eyes gleaming. "Let's bring him down. All the way down."

PATRICIA SAT AT THE CLUTTERED KITCHEN TABLE SURROUNDED by financial reports, scribbled notes, and a lukewarm cup of coffee she'd forgotten to finish. The late afternoon sun slanted through the window. Her phone buzzed violently against the glass top, jolting her out of her reverie. She snatched it up, glancing at the screen—BioTech Labs. Her pulse quickened. This was it.

"Hello?" she answered, her voice steady despite the nervous flutter in her chest.

"Ms. Falcon? This is Dr. Eric Hensley from BioTech Labs," came a measured voice on the other end. "I'm calling about that rush analysis requested on your infusion sample."

Patricia gripped the phone tighter. "Yes, thank you for getting back to me so quickly. What did you find?"

"Well," Hensley began, his tone shifting to one of mild curiosity, "it's not what I expected, I'll tell you that. The sample you sent us is mostly distilled water. The remainder is a trace of safrole. That's it."

"Safrole?" Patricia frowned, scribbling the word onto a notepad. "What's that?"

"It's a natural compound, technically an organic molecule. Chemically, it's 1,3-benzodioxole-5-yl-1-propene, if you want the jargon. You'll find it in small amounts in things like sassafras oil or certain spices. It's got a faintly sweet, spicy smell—think root beer, if you've ever had the real stuff. But here's the kicker: the concentration in your sample is minuscule. We're talking maybe a few milligrams per liter. Harmless."

Patricia's mind raced. "So it's not some experimental cancer drug?"

Hensley let out a short, dry laugh. "Not even close. There's no evidence—none that I'm aware of, anyway—that safrole has any cancer-fighting properties. Back in the sixties, the FDA banned it as a food additive after some studies showed it caused liver tumors in rats, but that was at doses thousands of times higher than what's in your sample. What you've got here? It's essentially a drop in the bucket. It wouldn't cure a cold, let alone cancer."

Patricia's pen paused mid-scrawl. She felt a slow, triumphant grin spreading across her face. "So you're saying this infusion drug, it's just water with a pinch of this safrole? Nothing therapeutic?"

"Exactly," Hensley replied. "I ran it through gas chromatography-mass spectrometry myself to be sure. No other active compounds, no trace of anything that could remotely qualify as a chemotherapeutic agent. It's a sham. If someone is selling this as a treatment, he's either delusional or a con artist."

A surge of satisfaction warmed Patricia's chest. After weeks of digging, interviewing desperate patients and former employees, piecing together Gryoti's vague promises of revolutionary infusions, and obtaining a sample, she finally had it. Proof. Cold, hard, lab-certified proof that his so-called miracle cure was nothing but a glorified bag of flavored water.

"That's incredible," she said, barely containing the excitement in her voice. "I mean, not incredible for his patients, of course. But thank you, Dr. Hensley. This is exactly what I needed."

"No problem. I'll have a certified lab report drafted up with all the details—chemical breakdown, concentration levels, the works. If you're taking this to someone official, it'll hold up. We're accredited, and I'll sign off on it myself."

"Perfect," Patricia said. "I can't tell you how much I appreciate the rush on this."

"Happy to help. Just be careful. People don't fake cancer treatments for fun. The oncologist using this has to know he's on thin ice."

"I'll watch my back," she promised, though her thoughts were already spinning with the thrill of the chase. "Thanks again, Dr. Hensley."

"Anytime. Good luck, Mrs. Falcon."

The call ended with a soft click, and Patricia set the phone down on the table, leaning back in her chair. She stared at the ceiling, letting the weight of the moment sink in. Safrole in distilled water. No cancer-fighting ability. A certified lab report on the way. She had Gryoti. After all the dead ends, the threats, the gnawing doubt—she'd cracked it wide open.

She reached for her coffee, took a sip, and grimaced at the cold bitterness. Didn't matter. She felt too good to care. Gryoti's house of cards was about to come tumbling down, and she was the one swinging the wrecking ball.

CHAPTER 31

First thing the following morning, Patricia sat in her bathrobe at her massive oak desk in her office, which was steeped in the soft glow of early morning. Through the two tall windows draped with lace sheers, she caught a glimpse of Falcon Square, where wandering pathways wound around huge azalea bushes and ancient oaks, their limbs draped with Spanish moss swaying gently in the morning breeze.

The air carried the familiar scent of old leather from the black leather high-back chair behind her and the pair of matching chairs arranged in front of the fireplace. The rich oak wood floor, partially hidden by an antique Persian Sarouk rug, muted the sounds of the awakening city outside. Despite the serene surroundings, a palpable tension lay beneath the surface as Patricia launched into another long day in her relentless investigation.

To start, she placed a call to Algenon. She knew he normally got to the office early. The phone call to update him on her investigation was brisk and focused—a well-rehearsed prelude to the day's unfolding challenges. As she spoke, the gravity of the case bore down on her, a turbulent blend of determination and a few lingering unanswered questions clouding her thoughts.

"Great work, Patricia," Algenon said, his voice both reassuring and businesslike.

"Thank you," she replied, her tone steady as she glanced briefly at Trey's photo in its simple silver frame; a reminder of the legacy and the stakes involved. "We've got more work to do to define Gryoti's financial network, and I need your help to dig into his crypto transactions. We've recorded proof that he claims his infusions work, and certified lab evidence points to the so-called drug being nothing more than flavored water. With this proof, I suspect there's sufficient probable cause to secure a warrant for his crypto records. Could you do that for us?"

"Of course," Algenon responded without hesitation. "But I'll need the supporting documentation. Could you send me a transcript of the Gryoti conversation and a copy of the lab report as soon as possible?"

"I'll get that to you immediately," Patricia affirmed, her mind already racing ahead to the next steps. The soft clack of her fingers on the desk's surface blended with the low hum of the early morning. "On a different matter—and this is where it gets more complicated—based on Gryoti's long history of intimidation and strong-arm tactics, I suspect he might have been involved in the death of your agent who was investigating him five years ago."

"Peter Dorsey?" Algenon said, his voice laced with a mixture of disbelief and grim recollection.

"Yes. Him. And while we're on the subject, what do you have on the truck driver who crashed into Dorsey's car?" Patricia pressed, her tone growing more urgent.

"Let me see," Algenon murmured, the soft tapping of keys audible as he scanned through his database. "Okay, here it is.

Marcus Pine. He wasn't much help in our investigation. In fact, he died shortly after the accident."

"Do you have a coroner's report on his death?" she asked, the pace of her speech quickening with anticipation, as if every second brought them closer to an elusive truth.

"Give me a moment," he replied. After a brief pause that stretched just long enough for suspense to build, he continued. "Hmm. It appears he died of an overdose of safrole."

At that revelation, Patricia's heart skipped a beat. "Gryoti has a long history of researching safrole," she said, each word deliberate and heavy with implication. "And he uses a trace amount of it in his fake cancer drug. This isn't just a coincidence."

"I agree, Patricia," Algenon replied. "I'll open an investigation into Pine's death. And check to see if there's any evidence of a connection between Gryoti and Pine—perhaps even a financial payoff or a hidden partnership that could explain the chain of events."

As they continued discussing the finer points of the investigation, Patricia's gaze drifted back to the window. The delicate lace sheers softly filtered the burgeoning light, casting intricate shadows on the Persian rug. Outside, Falcon Square was slowly coming to life, its pathways and azalea bushes bathed in the gentle radiance of a bright new day. In that moment, a renewed sense of purpose surged within her. The weight of secrecy and deception, though ever-present, seemed a little less oppressive against the backdrop of progress and clarity.

"Thanks, Algenon," she said, her voice imbued with both gratitude and steely determination. "I'll forward you the documents right away, and you can take it from there. There appears to be a much larger picture here than just medical fraud."

The conversation ended with a promise of continued

collaboration and a firm commitment that they remained united in their quest for justice and truth. As Patricia set her phone down, she took a deep breath, bolstered in her resolve for the challenges that lay ahead.

Patricia headed to the home gym, her mind racing with everything she'd learned. She set the treadmill to a steady pace, hoping the rhythmic thudding of her sneakers against the belt would help her process it all. Thirty minutes later, sweat glistening on her forehead, she slowed to a cool-down walk, then headed to the bathroom. A hot shower helped loosen the tension in her shoulders, but her mind remained sharp, focused.

Back in her office, she settled into her chair, brushing damp hair away from her face as she reached for her phone. The moment she dialed, Isabel answered, her voice bright.

"Good morning, Isabel. How are you doing?"

"I'm doing fine." There was warmth in her tone, but Patricia could sense a hint of exhaustion beneath it.

"And Lucius?"

A pause. "Not so good. He's having a bad day—fatigue, bone pain, brain fog." Isabel sighed softly, the weight of worry evident in her voice. "I just made double fudge brownies, his favorite. Hopefully, they'll lift his spirits."

Patricia smiled, picturing Isabel in her kitchen, the rich aroma of chocolate filling the air. "Should he see a doctor?"

"Normally, these episodes go away on their own in a day or two," Isabel explained. "If not, we'll schedule an appointment."

"Sounds good." Patricia hesitated, then took a deep breath. "I called to let you know we got back the lab results of the drug sample." She let the words settle for a beat before continuing. "The infusion drug Magnum is giving Lucius is nothing more than flavored water. It has no cancer-fighting characteristics at all."

Silence. Then Isabel exhaled sharply. "Finally, a definite answer. Thank you, Patricia."

"You're welcome."

"Father is infuriated over Gryoti's scam," Isabel admitted. "He's eager to sue the man for damages."

Patricia leaned forward, gripping the edge of her desk. "Please slow Lucius down," she cautioned. "With the lab results, we have solid proof of Gryoti's malpractice, but to completely take him down we need to locate his assets and confirm his partners before bringing him in. We have some strong leads on where he's putting his money, and some financial pros are tracking down his far-reaching financial network." She let that sink in before adding, "If Lucius could hold off suing until we complete the financial investigation, we stand a better chance of finding what he's stashed away. Money that can go to his victims. We don't want to tip Gryoti off about how much we know."

"I'll let Father know," Isabel said.

"Thank you, Isabel. We want to do everything possible to take Gryoti down once and for all."

"So do we, Patricia. If we can help in any way, please let us know."

Patricia nodded to herself. They were closing in. And this time, there would be no escape for Gryoti.

Shortly before noon, Simon knocked on the doorjamb of Patricia's office. The rhythmic clack of her keyboard paused as Patricia glanced up from her laptop, her sharp eyes narrowing slightly in curiosity. Sunlight streamed through the tall windows behind her, casting a warm glow on the stacks of case files and notes spread across her desk.

"Yes?" she said.

"Sorry for the interruption, but I think you'll want to see this." Simon motioned toward the dining room.

Patricia saved her work with a decisive click before

pushing back from her desk. "Alright," she said, rising gracefully.

She followed Simon down the wide hall, the polished hardwood floors creaking faintly beneath their steps. Entering the dining room, the grand crystal chandelier overhead caught the midday sun, scattering pinpricks of rainbow hues onto the dark wood paneling. A faint scent of beeswax polish filled the air.

Simon gestured toward his laptop and two external monitors set up on the table, their screens glowing softly in the otherwise warm, natural light.

Patricia settled into a chair, the upholstered seat cushion cool as she crossed one leg over the other. "What am I looking at?"

Simon tapped a few keys, and the screen refreshed, displaying a list of local properties with value figures in the millions beside them. "Gryoti's real estate investments. A total value of just under fifty million and largely paid off."

Patricia's brow lifted slightly. Her gaze flicked over the six properties listed on the screen, each worth a hefty seven-figure sum. "He owns these personally?"

"Shell companies," Simon said, allowing himself a rare, satisfied smile. "A complex network with multiple layers. It's taken me a week to put it all together."

Patricia leaned in slightly, studying the intricate connections Simon had mapped out. "I was wondering why I hadn't heard much from you. Every time I walked down the hall, you had your head buried in your computer."

He nodded, clicking to another screen. "The web spiders I released a week ago brought back a lot of the same data you originally had, but they also picked up some anomalies—strange links that led me to these shell companies. It took time to untangle them because several of these entities exist solely to own other shell companies. But eventually, I got to this list of real estate holdings."

She exhaled, shaking her head. "How did Gryoti buy this much real estate?"

"I checked with Meredith. The original shell companies I found appear on Gryoti's books as suppliers. Every month, he writes them sizable checks and categorizes the payments as expenses."

Patricia's lips pressed into a thin line. "Money laundering?"

"Without question. Classic money laundering."

"And they're mostly paid off?"

"All but one—his most recent purchase. He has about a million left on that one. At the rate he's writing checks to these shell companies, he should have that mortgage paid off within a year."

Patricia drummed her fingers against the polished wood as she considered the implications. "Great work, Simon."

"Thank you. Oh. I also installed the upgraded security features on the garage and doors. When you have time today, I need you for a few minutes to set up the retina identification system."

She pushed back from the table. "Let's do it right now."

CHAPTER 32

*P*atricia arrived at the Gryphon Tea Room well before her three p.m. meeting with Dr. Demetri Gryoti. A meeting he had requested. The choice of venue had been hers. Neutral ground, yet elegant, a public place where any aggression would attract attention. The scent of bergamot and fresh scones lingered in the air, blending with the quiet murmur of conversation and the occasional chime of silverware against porcelain. The rich mahogany bookshelves lined with aging tomes lent the space a scholarly air, while the soft glow of Tiffany lamps cast patterns across the white-clothed tables.

For safety's sake, Simon arrived soon after and took a table close to the door, positioning himself where he could see both Patricia and any potential threats. He sipped a coffee and pretended to read a book, though his sharp eyes flicked up every few moments.

At exactly three p.m., Gryoti entered. He wasn't alone. A broad-shouldered man in a tailored charcoal suit—easily recognizable as a bodyguard—paused in the lobby, scanning the room with the detached vigilance of someone accustomed to violence. Patricia hadn't seen a bodyguard with Gryoti at the gala. That meant either he felt vulnerable now, or the guard was here to send a message.

Leaving the bodyguard in the lobby, Gryoti approached her table with practiced grace, his navy suit crisp, his red silk tie a stark contrast against his white shirt. His combed-back wavy gray hair gleamed under the ambient lighting, and his striking blue eyes locked onto hers with something between amusement and calculation. On his right hand, he wore a gold signet ring, the crest indistinct but undoubtedly meaningful, and a vintage Omega watch-a collector's piece that hinted at both wealth and vanity.

Patricia stood as he reached the table.

"Thanks for meeting with me," he said smoothly, extending his hand. His grip was firm but not aggressive, his skin cool.

She shook his hand briefly, then motioned for him to sit.

A waiter appeared almost instantly. They both ordered water. No tea. No pretense of civility.

Patricia studied him, leveling her gaze at his expressionless face. "So, what do you want to talk about?" Her tone was flat, unyielding. She noted the slight shift in his posture, the almost imperceptible narrowing of his eyes. He hadn't expected her to be that direct.

"A business proposition," he said, lacing his fingers together.

"Really?"

"You've been speaking with some of my former patients, digging up unsubstantiated claims regarding my practice. And you've ignored my requests to stop."

Patricia held up a hand. "You're behind the notes and the break-ins?"

His lips curled into a humorless smile. "You know I am." He lifted his water glass and took a deliberate sip before setting it down with a quiet clink against the tabletop. "I'd like to incentivize you to stop your investigation. How does a million sound?"

She leaned back in her chair, letting the tension build, watching him as a predator watches prey. "You sound desperate."

His smile thinned. "Just thinking about my future."

"We both know you have no future if those allegations can be proven."

His fingers tapped rhythmically against the table. "You want more to stop investigating? Name your price."

"Justice is not for sale today."

His voice sharpened. "Are you sure about that?"

"Are you threatening me?"

He shook his head slowly, exhaling as if in disappointment. "I'm just discussing business. Are you interested in doing business with me? I could put the money in a foreign account, far from prying eyes."

"I've already given you my answer."

Gryoti tilted his head slightly, studying her the way one might assess a chessboard, calculating his next move. "Would you prefer a lawsuit? I'm sure my lawyer could come up with something that would bankrupt your family. No more fancy home. No more galas. No more Bentleys. The end of private school for your daughter."

Patricia remained still, keeping her expression unreadable. Beneath the jacket of her tailored suit, her phone was recording every word.

Gryoti's face darkened, his patience unraveling. "And if you don't care about wealth…" He let the sentence hang in the air, then leaned forward slightly. "Well. What can I say? Accidents happen."

Patricia's pulse remained steady. If he thought intimidation would break her, he was mistaken.

"Did you kill Pete Dorsey?" she asked, watching for the flicker, the tell.

Gryoti hesitated for a fraction of a second, then he shrugged. "He didn't listen to reason. Just like you." Gryoti picked up his glass again, rolling the water inside before taking another sip. "Are you sure you don't want to take me up on my offer?"

Patricia laughed. She had him.

"You appear desperate, Demetri," she said, her voice velvet-edged steel. "Which tells me the allegations from your practice are accurate."

He exhaled sharply through his nose, the muscles in his jaw tightening. "You have nothing on me," he said, pushing back from the table. "And you never will."

"I don't," she lied smoothly. "But I might in the future. And when I do, I'll see you in court."

His chair scraped against the floor as he stood. Across the room, his bodyguard straightened, his movements sharp, controlled, waiting for a cue.

But Gryoti gave none. His frustration simmered beneath his composed exterior as he turned on his heel and stormed out of the tearoom.

Patricia exhaled slowly. She had everything she needed, and Gryoti had no idea.

A waiter removed Gryoti's service with efficient precision, then turned to her with a polite smile. "Would you care to order?"

She hesitated for only a moment. The meeting had been intense, and she needed time to process everything. There was no rush. Better to sit, reflect, and sift through the layers of subtext in what had just transpired.

"Earl Gray tea and cranberry scones, please," she said.

As the waiter nodded and stepped away, she removed her phone from her jacket pocket and checked the recording.

The voices were clear—Gryoti's low, deliberate tone, her own measured responses, and the subtle shifts in cadence that hinted at things left unsaid. Pleased with the clarity, she opened her notes app and set the phone down on the table, ready to document anything she might have missed in the moment.

Across the room, Simon caught her eye. She gave him a slight thumbs-up. No doubt he had seen her check her phone. He would understand what that meant—the conversation had been captured in full. Another piece of evidence to add to the growing case.

She leaned back in her chair, allowing herself a moment of stillness as she replayed the meeting in her mind. Gryoti had been controlled, careful. That was expected. What was surprising were the specific omissions in what he chose to say. He had measured every word, every glance, every pause. The only real insight came from what was left out.

He was aware she had spoken with some of his patients. That much had been clear from the way he had steered certain topics, testing to see what she already knew. But he hadn't mentioned her conversations with his former employees. That was an interesting gap. Had he deliberately avoided bringing them up? Did he assume their perspectives were irrelevant? Or was he simply unsure how much she had uncovered? Did he know she had spoken to them at all?

Hard to tell, and best not to underestimate him.

He also hadn't mentioned Judy's apprehension. That was perhaps the most telling omission of all. Judy had been his enforcer. Ruthless, precise, and utterly loyal.

The bodyguard he had brought to the meeting suggested he wasn't lacking in security, but Judy must have been different. If she had been just another pawn, easily replaced, why hadn't Gryoti dismissed her loss outright? Why not acknowledge her downfall?

And if he knew about Judy's arrest, then he knew about Patricia's involvement in the arrest. Yet that hadn't come up either. That, too, was deliberate. It meant he was holding something back.

Ellery Hampton wasn't brought up either. Had he truly failed to make the connection between her and Ellery? That seemed unlikely. Gryoti was sharp. He didn't leave things to chance. Which meant he either didn't know or was pretending not to know. Either way, it was leverage.

Also, no mention of Meredith. That was another odd oversight—if it was an oversight at all. Why not acknowledge all three of them? Why not attempt to neutralize the threat with a single move? Yet, as far as she knew, he had only offered her a bribe.

It suggested he didn't see the full picture. But it also revealed something else: he wasn't aware of the extent of their collaboration. If he knew, he would have come at them differently—harder, more aggressively. Or with a broader offer. Instead, he had only dangled one incentive in front of her.

Which possibly meant he was operating with limited information. And that was an advantage.

Willie, Algenon, and Simon's investigations hadn't even been hinted at. Gryoti's silence on those fronts were another indication his knowledge was incomplete. That, or he was confident he had those angles covered. But if he had been as thorough as he liked to pretend, wouldn't he have at least tried to feel her out about those?

No. He had only targeted what he thought was the greatest risk to him. And he had miscalculated.

She took a slow, deliberate bite of the scone. Heavenly.

Life was good. And justice would soon be served.

CHAPTER 33

Gryoti exited the Gryphon Tea Room like a man emerging from battle. The confrontation had been clean. Civil. Lethal.

But she had refused.

He walked slowly, letting the cool November air slide past him like judgment. Inside, he boiled.

He had offered her a way out. He had given her an outstretched hand.

And she spat on it.

He stopped beside a wrought iron bench, the cast shadows tangled like roots at his feet. His heart was pounding—not with fear, but rage. Patricia Falcon didn't understand who she was dealing with. Didn't understand what he'd built. The reach he had. The people who owed him.

He sat. Reached into his coat pocket. His fingers closed around the old signet ring. His father's. A man who had come to America with nothing but pride and a will of iron.

She wanted war?

So be it.

He dialed a number.

"Carol," he said softly. "It's time. She won't back down. So we'll make her vanish."

A pause. Then a confirmation.

He ended the call and leaned back. Overhead, the blue sky was barely visible through the thick oak canopy.

But he could see clearly now.

No more games. No more warnings.

Only consequences.

Mid-morning sunlight filtered through the tall windows of Patricia's office. Outside, Falcon Square lay in quiet splendor. The view was as serene as ever, but inside her office, tension coiled in Patricia's chest like a snake ready to strike.

She sat behind the massive oak desk, its smooth surface cool beneath her fingertips. A symbol of stability and tradition. But at this moment, stability felt like a distant luxury. A crisp, cream-colored envelope lay before her—the notice of a defamation lawsuit that had just been served. Ten million dollars in damages. Patricia exhaled sharply, pushing the paper away as if it might sting her.

Her phone buzzed. She snatched it up, already anticipating what was coming.

Meredith had been served as well.

Meredith sounded composed, unsurprised even, as she assured Patricia that Gryoti's lawsuit wouldn't hold up. But when Ellery's name flashed on the screen next, Patricia braced herself.

"I just received notice of a million-dollar lawsuit against me."

"Don't worry, Ellery," Patricia said, trying to sound reassuring despite the gnawing frustration in her gut. "Anyone can bring a civil lawsuit with the flimsiest of evidence. The bar is low. Until we see what Gryoti has to back up his claim, we just respond within the deadline with a motion to dismiss. With any luck, we'll have Gryoti in jail before this ever goes to trial."

Ellery's voice wavered. "I can't afford to defend myself."

Patricia's grip tightened on the armrest. She heard the panic in Ellery's words, the weight of the legal battle pressing down on her. "Don't worry," she said, her voice firm. "We'll take care of that. We'll get you the best possible lawyer to guide you through the process."

There was a soft, grateful exhale. "Thank you," Ellery murmured. "I'll find a way to repay you."

"You're welcome. We're not going to allow Gryoti to intimidate us. And don't worry about repayment. Putting Gryoti away will be payment enough, you've been vital to that effort. By the way, did you have any success securing details on Gryoti's Bahamas accounts?"

"Yes. He has two accounts in the Bahamas. One feeds the other. The second account seems to be where Gryoti has amassed his financial assets—just over twenty-five million there. There has been no withdrawal from that account for over a decade. I should be receiving details on both accounts later today or tomorrow. And he owns an oceanfront condo in the Bahamas as well."

Patricia tapped her fingers lightly against the desk. That kind of money sitting untouched meant something. It meant patience. It meant confidence. And it meant Gryoti had a lot more to lose than just his livelihood.

When she ended the conversation with Ellery, Patricia

called Trey. He answered on the first ring. She told him about receiving the lawsuit notice.

"He sounds desperate," Trey said.

Patricia swiveled slightly in her chair, glancing toward the fireplace. How many late nights had she spent in this room piecing together the truth about Gryoti?

"I was thinking the same thing," she admitted. "So what do we do?"

"As for the defamation case, telling the truth isn't defamation. So we file a motion to dismiss and seek sanctions against the plaintiff."

Patricia sighed, rubbing her temple. "What about Ellery's case? She can't afford a lawyer."

"We can take care of that for her. Our strategy there will probably be to delay, delay, delay. We have lots of options to do that."

A flicker of relief loosened the tightness in her chest. "Sounds good," she said. "What's the next step?"

"I need copies of both notices."

"I'll let Ellery know. Love you."

"Love you too."

As soon as the call ended, Patricia turned her attention back to her desk. The desk lamp beside her cast a warm glow over the legal document, making the inked words feel even heavier. She reached for her phone and called Ellery again to request a copy of the notice for Trey.

"I'll do that as soon as we finish the call," Ellery promised. Then, after a brief hesitation, she added, "Now that we've located Gryoti's assets, maybe it's time to go on the offensive."

Patricia straightened in her chair. "What do you have in mind?"

"When I was in the DEA, at this stage, we'd get a warrant to seize drug samples, computers, and business files. And we'd seek to freeze the defendant's assets. Do you think I should contact the local DEA with what we know?"

Patricia considered it, glancing once more at Falcon Square outside. The Spanish moss swayed gently in the breeze, indifferent to the storm brewing in her life.

"I think we have all that we're going to find," she said finally. "Let's do it."

"Okay. Once the warrants are set up, I'll get back to you. If not this afternoon, first thing tomorrow."

After ending the call, Patricia sat in silence. The weight of the lawsuits, the schemes, and the relentless fight ahead settled over her. But there was something else, too, something more powerful than the threats against her.

Momentum. The wheels of justice had begun turning, and Patricia was eager to see them through.

She sat tapping a pen lightly against the desk's edge as she went over the case against Gryoti. A faint scent of old leather rose from the bookcases lining the walls, mingling with the smell of aged paper and the lingering smoke from last night's fire in the hearth.

Her phone vibrated. Meredith. Patricia picked up.

"Hey, Meredith."

"I just wanted to update you on Gryoti's use of cryptocurrency," Meredith said, her voice sharp and businesslike, though Patricia could hear the hint of fatigue beneath it.

Patricia leaned back, eyes flicking toward the window, watching a young couple stroll hand in hand along one of Falcon Square's paths. "And?"

"As far as I can tell, he was late to the crypto game and not very sophisticated at it."

"Easy to track?"

"Nothing about crypto detection is easy," Meredith admitted. "But with Algenon's warrants and some very effective tools, we found what we were after. Gryoti wasn't good at washing his transaction trail. He didn't even use the privacy coins with enhanced anonymity—just stuck with the big three cryptocurrencies, chain-hopping across multiple blockchains."

Patricia frowned. "Sounds complex."

Meredith gave a short, dry laugh. "The simple version is that he currently holds two million in crypto."

Patricia let out a low whistle. "Great work."

"Thank you."

"When are you responding to Gryoti's lawsuit?"

"I've already contacted my attorney. He's filing for a dismissal."

"We're doing the same thing, and so is Ellery." Patricia absently spun her pen between her fingers. The lawsuits were just another move in a desperate man's endgame. "By the way, Ellery located Gryoti's accounts in the Bahamas. Plus, Simon tracked down his real estate holdings. Nearly seventy-five million between the two."

Meredith exhaled sharply. "Damn. That's more than I expected."

"Ellery thinks it's time to turn everything over to the DEA."

"Good move," Meredith said. "With what we have, they'll be able to take down Gryoti hard."

Patricia nodded, even though Meredith couldn't see her. She reached out and traced the edge of Trey's photo with her fingers. They had worked too long, too hard, for Gryoti to slip through their fingers now.

Around two, as the afternoon light casted shadows across the rug, her phone vibrated again. Trey's name flashed across the screen.

"Hey, Trey."

"I haven't received a copy of Ellery's notice. Could you remind her to send it to me?"

Patricia straightened. "That's strange. She's usually right on top of things. I'll give her a call right away."

After hanging up, she immediately dialed Ellery. The call went to voicemail. She left a message, then followed up with a text: *Call me ASAP.*

Patricia drummed her fingers on the desk, a sense of unease creeping in. Thirty minutes later, she called again. No answer. Patricia's gaze flickered toward the fireplace, where flames had crackled the night before. Now, only cold ashes remained.

Something wasn't right.

She got up from the desk and headed to the dining room, where Simon was at work.

Patricia stopped at the head of the cherrywood table. She had always found comfort in this room—the way the damask wallpaper's muted blue and gold tones felt both regal and soothing, the gentle flicker of electric flames dancing along the polished silver candelabras. But this afternoon, an unease settled deep in her chest, gnawing at the edges of her composure.

Simon sat across from her, his laptop open amid the refined elegance of the dining table, a jarring contrast between modern urgency and timeless tradition. He looked up. His fingers paused over the keys, his expression sharp with concentration.

Patricia clenched her fingers around the back of one of the ornately carved chairs, her nails pressing into the upholstery as she tried to steady her voice. "Ellery's not answering her phone, Simon. She always answers her phone. Could you check to see if it's on and, if it is, where her phone is?"

She slid a slip of paper with Ellery's number across the polished surface, the white paper stark against the rich wood grain.

"Sure. Give me a minute." His hands moved in a practiced

rhythm, keying in commands. The glow of the laptop screen cast a pale light on his angular face, deepening the worry etched between his brows. A moment later, an image flashed onto the screen. Then more typing.

"Yes," he said finally, his voice clipped, businesslike. "It's on. And it's at her home."

Patricia exhaled, but the breath did nothing to ease the knot of tension coiling in her stomach. "Ellery's watch is attached to that number. Even if she went out without her phone, my calls would go to her watch. I don't like this." She turned toward the grand fireplace, her gaze briefly catching the solemn eyes of the Falcon ancestor in the oil painting above the mantel. As if he, too, was watching, waiting.

She inhaled sharply. "Gryoti has threatened her. And he just filed a lawsuit against her." Her voice hardened at the name.

Simon sat back, his chair creaking softly, the only disruption in the tense quiet. "I can run over to her home and see if she and her car are there."

Patricia turned, her gaze locking onto his. "Okay," she said, her voice steady, determined. "But I'm going with you."

Simon studied her for a beat, perhaps considering an argument, but he must have seen the unwavering resolve in her expression. With a nod, he closed the laptop.

CHAPTER 35

Ten minutes later, they pulled up to Ellery's house. Her car sat undisturbed in its usual spot. The house itself loomed quiet and still, the air thick with an eerie hush.

Patricia's pulse kicked up as she stepped onto the porch. Something felt wrong. The house had an almost abandoned feel to it, the kind that sent a shiver up her spine. She pressed the doorbell. A chime echoed inside, fading into silence. No answering footsteps.

She knocked firmly. Then again, harder. The door rattled in its frame. Still nothing.

"Call her phone one more time," Simon said, his voice taut.

With fingers suddenly clumsy, Patricia punched in Ellery's cell number. A split-second later, a muffled ringtone floated from inside the house.

Her stomach twisted.

She turned toward the sidelight window and cupped her hands against the glass. There, just beyond the threshold, sat Ellery's purse, keys, and phone on the foyer table. The sight of them sent a fresh wave of unease rolling through her.

"Her purse and phone are here," she said. She met Simon's gaze, her worry mirrored in his tense expression.

Simon moved to the front window, scanning inside. "She's not in the living room. I'll check the back."

Patricia remained frozen on the porch as Simon disappeared around the side of the house. The seconds stretched into long, agonizing minutes. A steady drumbeat of anxiety pounded in her chest.

When Simon reappeared, his face was grim. "No sign of her in the kitchen or family room. No overturned furniture, no broken glass. If something happened, it wasn't violent."

Patricia wrapped her arms around herself, rubbing at the chill creeping up her spine. "I think we should call the police."

"They might be hesitant to make entry without any signs of violence," Simon said.

Patricia's jaw tightened. That wasn't good. She punched in a number and pressed the phone to her ear. "Maybe Chief Patrick can speed things up."

Chief Patrick agreed to send someone right over.

Minutes dragged by, each one pressing heavier than the last. Finally, a police car pulled to a stop in front of the house. Her friend Detective Alex Rodriquez stepped out, followed closely by a locksmith.

It took mere moments for the door to click open, revealing the shadowed interior of Ellery's home. Rodriquez turned to them. "Wait here." He stepped inside, his hand instinctively hovering near his holster.

Patricia's breath felt locked in her chest as she exchanged glances with Simon. Neither spoke.

Each passing second stretched unbearably.

When Rodriquez finally re-emerged, his face was unreadable.

"She's not here."

Patricia's heart sank. "She has no family locally," she said. "Can I file a missing person's report?"

Rodriquez gave her a steady look. "Already done." A beat of silence. "If you don't mind, Mrs. Falcon, I'd like ask you a few questions about Miss Hampton to help focus our investigation."

"Of course."

Rodriquez pulled out a small black notebook and a pen. "When did you last see Miss Hampton?"

"I spoke to her this morning."

"Do you know anyone who would want to harm her?"

"Dr. Demetrius Gryoti. He didn't like that we were investigating him for fraud. He threatened her."

The questioning continued for several minutes. "Thank you, Mrs. Falcon. If you can think of anything else that might help, please call me." He gave her a business card.

"Now what?"

"I'll check the morgue and the hospitals. Then I'll talk with Dr. Gryoti."

"How can I help?" she asked.

"We can handle it."

She knew Rodriquez was an excellent detective. She'd worked with him before. But her doing nothing? Patricia clenched her jaw. No, doing nothing was not an option. She turned to Simon as they walked back to his car, determination hardening inside her like stone.

Ellery was missing, and Patricia intended to find out why.

Patricia and Trey entered the family room after dinner, their footsteps softened by the plush rug that stretched across the hardwood floor. The marble fireplace, unlit but imposing, added a quiet elegance to the space, while the crystal chandelier cast a soft glow over the bookshelves lining the walls. The large casement windows revealed the faint shimmer of moonlight over the backyard.

Trey moved toward the sleek, built-in bar against the far wall. He reached for a bottle, tilting it toward her. "Wine?"

She hesitated before nodding. "Yes, please."

As he poured, Patricia pulled a thick lap blanket over her legs, tucking it around herself. The November chill had seeped into the house, making the room feel cavernous despite its warmth. She adjusted her position on the sofa, sinking into its comfort, but the tension in her shoulders refused to ease.

Trey handed her a glass of Chardonnay, the pale-gold liquid catching the chandelier's light. With his own glass in hand, he dropped onto the sofa beside her, the cushions shifting slightly beneath his weight. His dark eyes studied her. "How are you doing?"

She exhaled, staring into her wine. "I'm troubled."

His brows lifted. "What's wrong?"

"Ellery's missing," she said, gripping the stem of her glass. "We were just wrapping up our investigation, and now she's gone." Her voice cracked slightly, the fear she had tried to suppress pushing to the surface.

He leaned forward, placing his glass on the coffee table. "Did you call the police?"

"Yes."

"And?"

She set her wine glass down beside his. The simple motion felt heavy, final, as though placing the glass down acknowledged the reality of her growing dread. "The police are on it, but my friend—a person helping me investigate a killer—is missing."

Without hesitation, he reached for her hand, his warmth grounding her. "How can I help?"

She swallowed hard. "Just be here with me while I try to figure out what to do."

He gave her hand a gentle squeeze. "We."

She turned to him, puzzled. "What?"

"While *we* figure it out."

Something in his voice—a quiet certainty, an unwavering loyalty—broke through the tightness in her chest. The fear didn't vanish, but it softened at the edges. She scooted closer, leaning into him. His arm curled around her shoulders, steady and strong.

"Oh, bless you, Trey," she whispered, closing her eyes for a moment.

As comfortable as cuddling with Trey was, Patricia couldn't shake the unease creeping through her chest. Ellery could be hurt, trapped, or worse. Every second wasted felt like a step closer to the worst possible outcome.

She sat up, her pulse quickening. "Our first priority in finding Ellery is checking the morgue and hospitals."

"The police will do that." Trey's voice was calm, but there was an edge to it.

Patricia exhaled sharply. "Okay. Let's assume she's alive and not in a hospital. Our next priority—what if she's a hostage?"

Trey rubbed his jaw. "The police will check her security videos."

"She doesn't have security." Patricia's hands curled into fists. "And we don't need them. Let's assume Gryoti or one of his thugs abducted her. Where would they take her? Somewhere close. He's not dumb enough to use his home, but it has to be somewhere he can sneak a hostage into without attracting attention."

Trey's brow furrowed. "Didn't you say he owns six properties in Savannah?"

"Yes. They're big and scattered all over the city. How do

we check them all before Gryoti does something drastic? We don't have much time."

Then it hit her. Her breath caught. "Wait. That's it. Time. Her watch. She never takes it off." Her heart pounded as she jumped up and sprinted upstairs.

She rapped on the door of the guest room where Simon was staying.

The door flew open. Simon stood there, half-dressed, eyes sharp. "Yeah?"

"We need you to locate Ellery's watch."

"No problem. As long as the 'Find Me' feature is on, and the watch is connected to a network." He threw on a black tee-shirt.

Minutes later, they were huddled around Simon's laptop in the dining room. The screen flickered, then a blinking dot appeared on the map.

"There it is."

Adrenaline shot through Patricia's veins. "Let's go get her."

Trey hesitated. "The police should handle this."

She spun to face him. "And when they ask how we found her? When they dig too deep into your methods? Into Simon's? You really want that kind of attention?"

Trey sighed. "No." He glanced at Simon. "I think the three of us can handle it."

Simon was already strapping into his body armor. His movements were crisp, calculated. "From what I know about Gryoti, he's not big on armed security. Just muscle."

Patricia's stomach churned. 'Just muscle' didn't make it any less dangerous.

Upstairs, she and Trey armed themselves. When they regrouped at the back door, the weight of the weapon against her body felt heavier than usual.

"Let's take the Navigator," Trey said.

. . .

Twenty minutes later, Patricia pulled into an abandoned strip mall. Most of the lights in the parking lot were dark. Broken glass crunched under the tires as they rolled to a stop. No other cars. No signs of life. The place reeked of decay.

"Do you think they'd leave her unguarded?" Patricia whispered, her fingers tightening around the grip of her weapon.

Simon scanned the area, his face unreadable. "It fits Gryoti's style." He handed them comm devices.

"Where's our entry point?" Trey asked.

Simon pointed to a boarded-up restaurant.

Patricia's gut twisted.

"I'll take the front," Simon said. "Trey, you take the back. Let me know when you're in position."

Trey nodded. "Copy that." He moved from the SUV like a shadow, disappearing into the darkness.

Patricia turned to Simon. "What about me?"

"I need you here for overwatch. If someone shows up, we need a heads-up." His voice softened. "Keep the engine running."

She swallowed hard and nodded. "Okay."

Simon slipped out of the Navigator.

The silence stretched, thick and suffocating. She slid her hand in her purse and touched Gryoti's gold money clip for luck.

Then Trey's voice crackled over comms. "I'm in position."

Simon placed a charge on the door. Moments later, the explosion of the restaurant door lock sent Patricia's heart slamming into her ribs. A flashbang followed—bright, deafening. Simon entered. Then nothing.

The seconds stretched.

Then—

"Found her," Simon's voice rang through the earpiece. "Coming out."

Patricia gripped the steering wheel so hard her knuckles ached. Then she saw them—Simon first, rifle raised, sweeping the lot. Then Ellery, stumbling, dazed but alive. Trey was right behind them.

Patricia's eyes burned. *Alive.*

Simon shoved Ellery into the car, then followed her in. As soon as Trey had his door shut, Patricia accelerated.

Sirens erupted in the distance.

"Let's get out of here," Simon shouted.

She didn't need to be told twice.

CHAPTER 36

The flames licked higher.

Gryoti stood still in the center of his clinic. Bins of used vials, forms, confidential notes—anything damning—were burning. The scent was bitter: chemicals, scorched paper, charred legacy.

Carol monitored the process, quiet and expressionless.

He walked the corridor alone. Past infusion chairs. Past exam rooms. Each held memories—patients who had cried, begged, believed. He had given them hope. Sold them a dream. Some lived. Some didn't. All paid.

His office loomed ahead, empty now but for the essentials. Vanity wall bare. Naomi's photo the only thing left on the desk. He picked it up. Stared at her smile.

The gold cross at his throat pressed against his chest as he breathed. He touched it. A man of faith, in his own way. A god of a small domain.

Now, the god was being hunted.

He picked up a burner phone.

Spoke a phrase in Greek.

A man answered.

"Have the plane ready," Gryoti said. "I leave tonight."

He stepped back into the hallway. The firelight flickered behind him.

Everything was gone.

Except the will to survive.

And that, he knew, burned hotter than anything he'd left behind.

CHAPTER 37

For safety's sake, Ellery spent the night at Patricia's home. The following morning, they were up with the sun. They had a lot to do to wrap up the case against Gryoti.

Patricia made crab cake Benedict for their breakfast, the scent of buttery hollandaise and Old Bay seasoning mingling with the soft aroma of fresh-brewed coffee. They ate in relative silence, the weight of the investigation pressing heavily upon them.

Around eight thirty, Simon entered the kitchen. His usually composed expression was tight with concern.

"There's a serious fire in progress at Magnum Oncology," he announced. "It's taken down Magnum's network."

The room stilled as Simon returned to the dining room. The hum of the dishwasher filled the silence as Patricia and Ellery exchanged uneasy glances.

Shortly afterward, Meredith called, her voice tight with urgency. "Patricia, Gryoti just transferred all his local funds to his account in the Bahamas."

The statement hung in the air, thick and heavy like the

scent of burning beeswax when a candle snuffs out. Thunder rumbled in the distance.

Following the call, Patricia went to share the new information with Simon.

"Sounds like Gryoti could be on the run," Simon said as his fingers flew over his laptop keyboard. A new image flashed on one of the monitors he had on the table, its top serving as his command center. "Gryoti is definitely on the run. Both his phone and watch went offline at eight this morning." He typed another command, his jaw tightening. Another image appeared on a second monitor. "His car GPS is still at his home. No movement since he drove home last evening."

Patricia grabbed her phone. "Meredith, Gryoti seems to be on the run. Can you check his recent credit card activity?"

"Sure," Meredith replied. "Give me a minute."

Patricia set the phone on speaker, placing it on the table between a stack of files and a cooling cup of coffee. Ellery leaned forward. The thunder was closer now.

"Okay. I have it," Meredith said at last. "No transactions since yesterday at noon."

"If he's running and not using his credit card, how will he pay for things? Going on the lamb has to be costly." Patricia's voice carried an edge of frustration.

"He might have created a cash hoard for situations just like this," Simon speculated. "Did he withdraw any cash before closing out that local account, Meredith?"

The silence stretched, tension thickening the room.

"No," Meredith said finally. "No cash withdrawals in the last month."

"Looks like he had all the cash he needed readily available," Patricia muttered, rubbing her temples. Heavy rain erupted, pelting the windows.

"If he had cash tucked away, he could also have fake ID

and burner phones," Simon added, his gaze never leaving the screen.

"We need to let the DEA know he's going dark," Ellery said, pushing back from the table. "They can coordinate with local and international carriers, as well as border control. Can I borrow your phone, Patricia?"

Patricia nodded and completed the call with Meredith before handing the phone to Ellery.

Ellery contacted the local DEA office with the latest information, then returned the phone to Patricia.

"Where do you suppose he's going?" Patricia asked, glancing at Simon.

"If he's smart, he'll avoid airports and official border crossings," Simon replied.

"So if not there, where would he go?" Patricia pressed.

Ellery folded her arms. "A remote community with little surveillance. Rent a mountain cabin in North Georgia or someplace like that. Everything on a cash basis. Lie low to regroup. Grow a beard. Wear sunglasses. Baseball cap. Or go to a small beach town in Florida and rent a bungalow for cash. As long as he has plenty of cash, he has plenty of options."

"And when he runs out of cash?" she asked.

"By then, he will have made his way into Mexico or some other country where he can resume medical practice under a new identity," Ellery said. "He's probably fled before and knows the ropes. Didn't you say he faked most of his credentials?"

"Yes," Patricia said. "So what do we do?"

"We let the DEA track him down," Ellery said, though there was little satisfaction in her tone.

"What about all that money in the Bahamas?"

"We have an extradition treaty with the Bahamas. The

DEA will request a freeze on the accounts. If he shows up to make a withdrawal, he'll be arrested and extradited."

"So his only choice will be to start over," Patricia said.

"That's what I would do," Ellery admitted. "The sooner, the better. Probably in Mexico, where it's easier to get a medical license if you grease the right palms."

"Can we monitor for new oncology practices in Mexico?" Patricia asked.

"We can," Ellery said. "But if he's smart, he'll join an existing practice."

"And we know he's smart," Simon said.

"So what do we do?"

"We let the DEA do their job," Ellery said, her voice resolute.

For the second time in as many days, Patricia had been told to stand down and let the authorities handle the situation. And for the second time, she couldn't accept that course of action. The problem was, she didn't have a viable alternative.

Not yet.

Simon returned Ellery to her home following lunch.

After putting the lunch dishes in the washer, Patricia's energy nosedived despite having just eaten. Her short, fretful night and early morning awakening had taken its toll, but she forced herself to get moving. Gryoti was on the loose, and there was urgent work to be done.

She made peppermint tea and carried the mug into the family room, the tea's scent curling upward in a soothing swirl of warmth. The rain had ended. The marble fireplace stood silent, its cold, polished surface reflecting the glow from the afternoon sun. Two chairs sat arranged in front of it, their cushions plump and inviting, remnants of past conversations lingering in their folds.

Patricia set her tea on the coffee table in front of the sofa, then sank into its embrace. The fabric was cool against her skin, and she instinctively curled one leg beneath her, letting her body settle into the familiar comfort. She glanced toward the floor-to-ceiling bookshelves lining one wall, the spines of hundreds of books standing in orderly rows, their silent knowledge a reassuring presence.

Despite the brightness of the room—the crisp daylight now filtering in, the gleam of crystal, the warmth of well-loved furniture—exhaustion pressed against her. The contrast between the cheerful space and her depleted mood was almost jarring. She exhaled, rubbed her temple, and leaned back, closing her eyes.

The hum of the house faded into the background. The faint tick of the grandfather clock in the foyer, the distant chirp of birds beyond the casement windows, the occasional creak of settling wood. Slowly, she let her breath deepen, her chest rising and falling in steady rhythm.

Sleep came instantly.

When she awoke a half hour later, her mind was on Judy. As a fugitive, she had evaded authorities for three years. She had gone off the grid in Savannah, then started over in Savannah. If Judy could do it, why couldn't Gryoti?

All he needed was an employer who valued his services and was willing to pay him in cash. He had plenty of rich, devoted patients. He could start a concierge oncology practice for the most desperate—a quiet, under-the-radar business that could keep him afloat.

So while the authorities pursued their traditional methods to find Gryoti, she'd start locating his most satisfied patients to determine if Gryoti was still practicing. It would take time, and right now, she had plenty of time to finish the job. It was a plan—not a perfect one—but it satisfied her need to join the hunt for Gryoti.

She took a long, satisfying sip of the lukewarm peppermint tea, the taste lingering on her tongue, and gazed absently at the fireplace. The house felt still, wrapped in an afternoon hush. She closed her eyes again, letting the warmth of the tea settle in her chest, and drifted back into a sound sleep.

When Patricia awoke at four, a deep sense of clarity settled over her. Sleep had sharpened her mind, and the fog that had clouded her thoughts earlier was gone. She stretched, savoring the rare moment of peace, before glancing at the clock. At least an hour remained before Trey would be home. It was enough time to dive back into the work of locating Gryoti.

Rising swiftly, she made her way to her office, the familiar space grounding her in purpose. She booted her laptop up, fingers already poised over the keyboard. She navigated quickly through her start screen, selecting the Gryoti case files.

As the documents loaded, she leaned forward, studying the pattern of life Simon had compiled on Gryoti. Wherever Gryoti settled, he was bound to fall into familiar routines. People were predictable that way, creatures of habit no matter how much they tried to disguise it.

Gryoti, for instance. Though his medical career consumed him, he made time for companionship—always on his terms. He favored serial monogamy, never juggling multiple women at once, but never staying with one for too long. One year, maybe two, before he moved on.

Patricia frowned, her fingers tapping idly on the desk. His current girlfriend, Carol Alberta, had been with him for eleven months. That meant their relationship was nearing its expiration date. Would he try to maintain it while he hid, or would he sever ties and disappear completely? Either way, she needed to talk to Carol.

She jotted down Carol's name and contact information before scrolling further.

Another detail in Simon's document caught her eye. Gryoti was meticulous about his appearance. His lab coats were always freshly laundered and pressed—professionally, not at home. If he planned to stay in Savannah and continue practicing medicine under the radar, would he use the same laundry service? Possibly. Another thread to pull. She noted the name and contact details of the cleaners.

Her gaze flicked to another habitual detail—swimming. Gryoti swam laps daily. It seemed more than exercise for him; it was a ritual. It was the kind of habit he wouldn't easily abandon. Would he search for a new pool in Savannah? Likely.

Patricia opened a new document and began listing public pools in the area. Then she went further—condo complexes with indoor lap pools, heated outdoor pools, anywhere he might feel comfortable continuing his routine. She didn't need to find him everywhere, just one place. One misstep on his part, one moment where routine overrode caution, and she'd have him.

Her pulse quickened.

Gryoti was also a sailor. He owned a sizable sailboat, one he could live on indefinitely if he wanted to. What better way to disappear than to slip onto the water, free from the constraints of land, away from prying eyes?

She scribbled a note to check on his boat's status. If he planned to use it, it would need maintenance, supplies. That gave her another lead to follow.

She exhaled slowly, sitting back in her chair. Gryoti's new pattern of life on the run was taking shape, a web of behaviors and preferences that could be his undoing.

The clock on the wall ticked softly. It was time to stop for the day.

With a final glance at her notes, Patricia closed her laptop. Her muscles ached from sitting too long, but she ignored the discomfort, standing and stretching as she made her way down the hallway. The portraits of Trey's ancestors watched her with their solemn, painted gazes, lining the walls like silent sentinels of the past.

In the dining room, Simon was finishing up his work, his fingers moving over the keyboard with quiet efficiency. He looked up as she entered.

"Can you still get into Magnum's patient records?" she asked.

"Yes. They're in the cloud, not affected by the fire. Which, by the way, totally consumed the clinic."

Patricia's jaw tightened. The fire had destroyed any physical evidence left behind, making her search more complicated. But not impossible.

"Anybody hurt?" she asked.

"No. The fire started before anyone arrived."

"If you don't mind," she said, keeping her tone casual, "I'd like a list of his patients who are currently receiving treatment."

Simon's fingers flew over the keyboard. "No problem," he said as he typed. "Do you want me to print out a list for you or email it?"

"Email would be fine. Thank you."

He nodded, his focus already back on the screen.

Patricia turned and made her way to the kitchen. Trey would be home soon, and she needed to get supper started. But even as she moved through the motions, her mind was still turning, still piecing together the puzzle.

She was getting closer.

And Gryoti wouldn't see her coming.

CHAPTER 38

As was their custom, Patricia and Trey shared a bottle of wine after dinner. The soft glow of the dimmed lights cast a warm ambiance over the family room, the air rich with the scent of oak and spice from the wine. After settling beside her on the plush sofa, Trey turned toward her, his expression thoughtful.

"How's Ellery doing?" he asked, swirling the wine in his glass.

"She seems to have handled the abduction well," Patricia replied, her voice tinged with admiration. "Said she had experienced worse. We put together an evidence package for the DEA and sent it this morning. Simon took her home after lunch."

Trey nodded. "So, it's all in the DEA's hands now."

"Not completely." She leaned back against the cushions, the weight of responsibility pressing against her shoulders. She told him about the devastating fire at Magnum Oncology, Gryoti going dark, and the investigation she had planned in case he'd chosen to stay in Savannah.

Trey raised his wine glass to her, a glimmer of pride in his eyes. "Well done."

They clinked glasses, the delicate chime resonating in the quiet room. Patricia sipped her wine, but something unsettled her. A whisper of doubt, a nudge of intuition. Over the years, she had learned to trust those feelings. She placed her glass on the coffee table, leaned into Trey, and closed her eyes, letting her thoughts drift through the murky depths of strategy and deception.

Gryoti was brilliant, possibly brilliant enough to evade detection for years, just like Judy had. She had remained a shadow, always a step ahead. Patricia had to outsmart Gryoti. Rather than wait for him to repeat past habits, she had to actively lure him out of hiding with something he couldn't resist. But what? What did Gryoti cherish more than his safety?

He was a narcissist, a man who placed himself above all others. Except, perhaps, his daughter. He doted on Naomi. If she were in danger, would he risk exposure? Maybe. Maybe not. Baiting him had to be something more compelling, something that appealed to his ego as much as to his heart.

Patricia stared at the flickering candle on the table, the flame swaying as if whispering a secret. Then, as the background music shifted to a classical piano piece, it struck her like a thunderbolt. Naomi was a professional pianist.

Stage a recital. A once-in-a-lifetime performance no proud parent could refuse. A Lincoln Center recital.

She turned sharply toward Trey, her pulse quickening. "We have a way to get him."

He listened intently as she laid out the idea. When she finished, he nodded, his gaze unwavering. "It's brilliant."

The following morning, Patricia called a close friend—a Lincoln Center trustee—who immediately pledged support. Within a week, Naomi Gryoti was scheduled to perform a recital at the prestigious Wu Tsai Theater in the David Geffen Hall, and the DEA had obtained an arrest warrant for Gryoti.

THE NIGHT OF NAOMI'S RECITAL CARRIED AN ELECTRIC charge, an unspoken tension that stretched thin over the opulent concert hall. The DEA, NYPD, and Coalition operatives were woven seamlessly into the crowd, disguised as ushers, patrons, and event staff. They had the exits covered, the backstage watched, and the house peppered with eyes, both human and electronic. If Gryoti appeared, he wouldn't leave freely.

Patricia and Trey arrived early, their practiced calm concealing the coiled anticipation beneath. The lobby gleamed with polished marble, chandeliers casting golden halos over the audience as they trickled inside. Security was thorough—metal detectors, bag checks, even a sleek black Labrador trained for narcotics and explosives. Patricia let the sniffer dog pass her without reaction. They lingered in the lobby to witness Gryoti's arrest, but none came. Just before the event was to begin, they entered the theater and took their seats in the center of the fifth row.

The vast 2,200-seat hall was only half full. The empty seats added an eerie stillness, amplifying the quiet whispers of the crowd. Patricia scanned the rows, searching for anomalies. The Coalition had accounted for everything, but if Gryoti had slipped through, he had to be somewhere.

The performance began.

Naomi played beautifully, her fingers a blur of precision and emotion. The music held the audience captive, washing over them in haunting waves. But as Patricia watched and listened, her investigative instincts caught something else— something outside the melody.

Naomi kept glancing toward the left side of the first few rows. It was subtle, a flicker of movement between notes. A secret smile in the middle of her performance. Patricia kept watching and zeroed in on the recipient—a middle-aged man with sharp features and silver-streaked hair. He sat with impeccable posture, hands resting neatly on his lap, as if he belonged. His eyes never left Naomi.

Patricia's pulse quickened. Was this him? It didn't look like Gryoti—not the photos she had studied, not the ghost-like figure she had spent months chasing. But something about the way Naomi acknowledged him made Patricia uneasy. She leaned toward Trey.

"Third row, left side, silver-streaked hair. Naomi keeps looking at him."

Trey's gaze followed hers. "Doesn't match Gryoti's description."

"No," Patricia murmured. "But watch his body language."

The man never clapped at the end of pieces. Never shifted in his seat. He was there for Naomi and nothing else.

At intermission, the audience stirred, a low hum of conversation filling the hall as people rose from their seats. Patricia watched as the man stood, buttoned his jacket, and exited toward the grand lobby.

"I'm following him," she said, rising smoothly.

Patricia maneuvered through the dispersing crowd, keeping her distance. The man strolled through the lobby, seemingly unbothered. She noted everything—his casual pace, the way he avoided eye contact, how his shoulders squared when he sensed someone behind him.

Then he turned slightly, and their eyes met.

Patricia saw it in an instant. A flicker of recognition. A moment of hesitation.

He knew who she was.

The shift was subtle but unmistakable—his posture

tensed, his fingers curled slightly at his sides. Then, just as quickly, he pivoted toward the far exit.

Patricia lunged forward.

"Stop!"

He bolted, shoving past a couple descending the grand staircase. A waiter carrying champagne flutes yelped as the tray crashed to the floor. Patricia dodged past the spill, her heels clicking against marble as she closed the distance.

The man veered toward the side doors, but Patricia was faster. She grabbed the back of his jacket and yanked hard, sending him off balance. He stumbled, and before he could regain his footing, she had his arm twisted behind his back, pressing him against the nearest marble pillar.

"Got you," she hissed, breathing heavy against his ear.

He didn't answer, but the fight drained from him.

Then Trey was there, along with two Coalition agents who had picked up the disturbance. One of them moved to assist, but Patricia kept her hold firm, her adrenaline still coursing.

Trey crouched slightly, eyeing the man's face. Then Trey's expression darkened. "It's him," Trey said. "For sure."

The agent beside them confirmed it. "Facial recognition just hit. It's Dr. Gryoti."

Patricia's fingers tightened around his wrist. He had altered his appearance just enough to throw off anyone searching for him, just enough to slip past law enforcement. But he couldn't fool his own daughter. Naomi had been looking at him because she knew.

And so did Patricia.

As security escorted him away, Patricia exhaled, her heart still pounding.

For months, Gryoti had been a shadow, a whisper, a name just out of reach.

Now he was hers.

EPILOGUE

*A*fter a lengthy and highly publicized trial, Gryoti was found guilty of multiple federal offenses, including health care fraud, tax evasion, and money laundering. The prosecution presented overwhelming evidence of his unethical medical practices, which had endangered countless lives. He was sentenced to twenty years in federal prison, a verdict that brought relief to many of his former patients and their families.

Meanwhile, a separate state criminal trial in Georgia reached a nearly identical conclusion. In addition, a group of his former patients, many of whom had suffered severe medical complications due to his malpractice, successfully filed a class action lawsuit against him. As a result, each plaintiff received a substantial settlement from his seized assets, offering some financial restitution for the harm Gryoti had inflicted.

As legal battles continued, federal prosecutors brought murder charges against Gryoti for the death of Agent Pete Dorsey. A trial date had yet to be set.

Despite the chaos Gryoti had caused, Lucius found a

measure of stability. After switching oncologists, his cancer treatments became more effective, and his condition stabilized, offering him and Isabel a renewed sense of hope for the future.

Determined to prevent future victims from suffering at the hands of corrupt medical professionals, Patricia took decisive action. Using a portion of her inheritance, she founded and funded a nonprofit organization dedicated to investigating and exposing medical fraud throughout the Southeast. The foundation quickly gained traction, partnering with law enforcement and investigative journalists to hold unethical practitioners accountable.

One such journalist was Willie, whose relentless pursuit of the truth in Savannah led to an award-winning exposé detailing the full scope of Gryoti's fraudulent activities, medical negligence, and the devastating consequences for his patients. The explosive story garnered national attention, reinforcing the importance of watchdog journalism in exposing systemic corruption.

Enraged by the coverage, Gryoti attempted to sue Willie for libel, but the case was swiftly dismissed in court. Willie not only won his countersuit, but was also awarded monetary damages, which he generously donated to Patricia's foundation.

Once the dust finally settled, Patricia and Trey decided it was time to prioritize themselves for once. In need of rest, healing, and a fresh start, they embarked on a long-overdue vacation to Bali, leaving behind the ghosts of the past and embracing the promise of a brighter future.

THE END

SAVANNAH CHRISTMAS
COMING 2026

ONE

*P*atricia Falcon stood on the front porch of her historic Savannah home and watched her long-time friend and florist extraordinaire wrap pine garland around the last porch column. The sharp scent of pine filled the air.

"What do you think?" Sheila asked as she climbed down and stepped to the front doors where Patricia stood. Sheila, dressed in overalls, wore large hoop earrings and just a hint of makeup. Her wavy brunette hair flowed over her shoulders. Sunglasses were perched on her head. Her pale blue eyes twinkled. Sheila's team of decorators were finishing up the other columns.

"Festive, fresh and just what I had in mind." *I'll Be Home for Christmas* played from a home speaker behind Patricia. "By the way, would you and your crew care for some hot chocolate when you're done?"

"Sounds yummy, but we have a few more homes to decorate today."

"That's why I've prepared insulated travel cups and little baggies of cookies. It won't slow you down a second."

Patricia motioned just inside the front doors where she'd rolled out the bar cart.

Sheila chuckled. "You're the ultimate Southern hostess, Patricia."

Patricia missed her weekly teas with Sheila who, like everyone else, was extraordinarily busy from just before Thanksgiving to New Year's Eve. Once the holidays were over, they'd resume their teas. Patricia scanned the pine garlands draped on the wrought-iron fence at the curb and on the handrails leading up the porch steps with admiration. "It looks so festive, Sheila."

"Thank you." Sheila unwrapped a large red velvet bow and handed it up to the decorator who affixed it to the top of the column. "All done," she said with a broad smile.

A UPS truck stopped in front of Patricia's home and a young man bounced from the truck with a big box that he had to put down to open the gate in her fence.

Patricia plucked a cup of hot chocolate and a portion of cookies and met him halfway to the house, then exchanged her offerings for the lightweight package. "Thank you, Mike," she said.

"Thank *you*, Miss Patricia," he replied in a thick drawl, tipping his Santa hat and then returning to his truck.

Patricia checked the shipping label, noting it was another package for Trey, and it was from Savannah Sweets. No doubt a Christmas gift from one of his clients.

"We'll deliver your Christmas tree tomorrow morning," Sheila said as she picked up garland fragments and placed them in a garbage bag.

Patricia smiled. "This is the *most* wonderful time of year."

"Most certainly." Sheila returned the smile. "Someone should write a song."

Patricia chuckled.

"I'll see you tomorrow to help with the tree."

"Thank you, Sheila, for all you do to make our holidays so very special."

"It's my pleasure." Sheila took the stuffed garbage bag to her van, and her three-man team enthusiastically partook of Patricia's Christmas treats as she bade them all farewell.

A family of four dressed in red holiday sweaters stopped on the sidewalk, snapped a photo of Patricia's festively decorated house, making Patricia beam with pride. Beyond them, the wrought-iron fencing and lampposts of the city square across from her home were fully decorated with pine swag and bright red bows. And, just in time for the holidays, the white and pink camellias were starting to bloom.

Patricia carried the large box of sweets inside and set it in the living room. Other than the Christmas music, the house was quiet. Trey was at work and her daughter Hayley still had another week at school, followed by a week-long trip to Utah with her college ski club.

Patricia let out a long breath as she headed for the kitchen. It had been quite a year. Several abused women rescued. A few cases solved. Now the year was coming to a fitting end with holiday cheer and much gratitude for blessings.

Patricia's cell chimed an incoming call. She checked the screen. *Camila Rodriquez.* Though she didn't recognize the name, she accepted the call.

"Good morning, Mrs. Falcon," a woman's voice said, breaking with emotion. "This is Camila Rodriquez. You know my husband Alvaro? He's a detective with the Chatham Police Force. He said he's worked with you in the past."

"Oh yes. A fine young man. I worked with him on the Maywood Jackson case. Is everything alright?"

"He's been shot." Her voice caught. "Critical condition."

Patricia swayed with shock. "Oh, my word. I'm so sorry."

"They put him into a medically induced coma." She hesitated, breathing rapidly between sniffs. "He thinks the world of you, Mrs. Falcon. He told me if he was *ever* mysteriously injured or incapacitated, to call you and ask you to investigate."

"I'm flattered your husband thinks highly of me, but I'm sure the police will do a thorough investigation. They don't take a shooting of one of their own lightly."

"They're investigating, Patricia, but Alvaro said you always go well beyond a police investigation. Something isn't right. What if he was targeted? His killer could come back to finish the job. I need to keep my husband safe. And I need to get the shooter off the streets. Mrs. Falcon. Please." She sobbed out the last plea.

Patricia's heart went out to the distraught woman. She couldn't imagine how she'd feel if it were Trey who'd been shot. "Let me call and find out exactly what the police think happened. Chief Patrick is a good friend of mine. If there's anything I can do, I won't hesitate. Alvaro is a wonderful man, and I'm so sorry to hear this devastating news." Patricia grabbed pen and paper from the kitchen counter. "If you're up to it, I'd like to ask you a few questions."

"Of course."

Patricia put her phone on speaker and sat at her glass-topped kitchen table. Filtered morning sun from the bay window lit the spacious room. "When did the shooting occur?"

"Late last night."

"Do you know the exact time?"

"I don't know. But the police called me around midnight."

Patricia dated the page, then wrote *before midnight.* "Where did the shooting occur?"

"I don't know. Alvaro was found outside of the emergency room entrance by hospital staff."

So, someone, possibly the shooter or an accomplice, wanted Rodriquez to survive. That was a positive sign. If he was targeted no one would have taken him to the hospital. She made a note of Camila's response and a note to check with Chief Patrick to see if they'd reviewed the hospital security videos for last night. And to see if they had checked traffic videos from the roads leading to the hospital. "What was Alvaro working on, Camila?"

"A theft. It's a new case. Last week, the chief took Alvaro off his other cases and told him to focus on this one. Because of the people involved, the department has put a lid on this case. No press releases."

This gave Patricia pause. "I don't suppose Alvaro told you who was involved?"

"No. He didn't."

Hopefully the chief would enlighten Patricia on who the victim was. "Okay. What's your husband's cellphone number?"

Camila gave Patricia Rodriquez's number.

Patricia made a note to ask her friend Timnit Araya to get ping information on Rodriquez's phone for the day of the shooting. "Anything else I should know?"

"His gun and car are missing," Camila said.

Patricia noted the information. Her page of notes was filling up fast. "Which hospital is your husband in?"

"Falcon Memorial."

Good. He'd get excellent care there. Plus, it would make getting a copy of the security videos much easier. "Okay, Camila. If you think of anything else I should know, please don't hesitate to call me. Details matter however minor they might seem. I'll let you know what I find out and if the chief needs me."

"Thank you, Patricia."

Once the call was completed, Patricia called her friend, Collin Patrick, Savannah's Chief of Police.

"Good morning, Collin."

"Good morning, Patricia. What can I do for you today?"

"I'm so sorry to hear Detective Rodriquez, an acquaintance of mine, has been shot. His wife called me. How is he?"

"He's in critical condition. It's touch-and-go right now."

"His wife asked me to join the investigation into the shooting. But, before I commit, I wanted to check with you first."

"Your help would be nice, Patricia. You know how we feel about one of our own being shot. We can use all the help we can get. Murphy is the lead detective. Her case file is online." Collin gave Patricia a guest password to use to access Murphy's case file. He'd done it before on other cases she'd assisted with.

Patricia made a note. She hadn't worked with Murphy before. Didn't know anything about her. "Will you give her a heads up about me helping?"

"Sure will, Patricia. As soon as this call is over."

"So, what do you have so far on the shooter?"

The chief exhaled. "Nothing. But Rodriquez's department car and gun are missing. There's a high likelihood the shooter has them. We put out an all-points bulletin on his car and are trying to locate the vehicle through our automated license plate reader program and by the car's GPS, but we've come up blank so far."

"That's unusual."

"Yeah. I'd guess the person who stole his car knows how to deactivate the GPS."

"Common knowledge?"

"No, but probably readily available on the internet."

Patricia laughed. "You've got to love the internet."

"It's surprisingly simple to deactivate a vehicle's GPS. All it takes is a cheap GPS detection device. Then, once you locate the vehicle's GPS unit, you simply deactivate it by removing the battery."

"Rodriquez was dropped outside the Falcon Memorial ER. Have you checked hospital security and traffic videos?"

"I understand Murphy is getting warrants for those as well as data on his cellphone."

"Rodriquez was working a theft. What exactly was stolen?"

There was a long pause. "A rare manuscript. Details should be in his case file," Chief Patrick said. "You can use the same guest password to access his case file. And, Patricia, this is a highly sensitive case, so we're keeping this quiet."

Patricia knew, simply from her connection to the Catholic church and her investigation of Trey's kidnapping, how large and sometimes dangerous the antiquities market was. "I understand the sensitivity. Anything else?"

"No," the chief said. "Welcome aboard. And let me know when you'd like to be deputized," he added dryly.

End of preview of Savannah Christmas
Sign my for my new release newsletter at www. AlanChaput.com for an email notification when Savannah Christmas comes out.

BOOK CLUB GUIDE

SAVANNAH MED

Book Summary

When a wealthy Savannah attorney's cancer treatments fail mysteriously, his daughter turns to amateur sleuth Patricia Falcon for help. Patricia's investigation quickly uncovers disturbing signs of fraud, betrayal, and criminality at Magnum Oncology, led by the charismatic but corrupt Dr. Demetrius Gryoti.

As Patricia digs deeper, she faces mounting threats—not just to her own safety, but to her family's as well. In a city known for its beauty and history, Patricia battles a sophisticated medical fraud empire, confronts her deepest personal fears, and ultimately seeks justice—not just for one victim, but for them all.

Savannah Med blends Southern atmosphere, medical intrigue, and relentless suspense into a gripping story of truth, betrayal, and the price of fighting evil.

Discussion Questions

1. **Characters & Motivations**

- Patricia is driven by a strong sense of justice. How do her motivations evolve throughout the story?

- How does Patricia's fear of losing Trey shape her actions during the investigation?

- What do you think motivated Dr. Gryoti to start down his criminal path? Was it purely greed—or something more?

2. **Themes of Justice and Fear**

- *Savannah Med* explores the difference between moral justice and legal justice. Which is more important to Patricia? To you?

- How does Patricia's internal battle with fear mirror the external battle she faces against Gryoti?

- Discuss how personal loss and trauma influence different characters' sense of right and wrong (Patricia, Ellery, Beau).

3. **Medical Ethics**

- Do you believe Gryoti's early experimental treatments were ever intended to help people? Or were they always a scam?

- Would you, or someone you know, ever consider an unproven treatment if you were desperate enough? Why or why not?

4. **Setting & Atmosphere**

- How does the Savannah setting—historic, beautiful, yet shadowy—contribute to the tension of the story?

- Could this story have worked in another city, or is Savannah essential to the novel's mood and plot?

5. Secondary Characters

- Which secondary character made the strongest impression on you—Trey, Meredith, Timnit, or someone else? Why?

- Timnit faces a personal decision about loyalty versus opportunity. How does her choice deepen the novel's justice theme?

6. Plot & Suspense

- What moments in *Savannah Med* did you find the most suspenseful?

- Were you surprised by the reveal of Judy's involvement and her grudge against Patricia?

7. Broader Issues

- The novel hints at real-world problems: corrupt medical boards, patient desperation, fake charities, and political influence. Which of these did you find most disturbing?

- How can patients protect themselves from fraudulent medical practices in the real world?

AUTHOR NOTES

Why Savannah?

There's no place like Savannah for a mystery. Cobble-stone streets, moss-draped oaks, secret courtyards, and a storied past—it's a city that whispers secrets at every turn. In *Savannah Med*, I wanted to show both its beauty and its shadows. Patricia Falcon lives in a historic home in the heart of the city, and her investigations often take her into real neighborhoods, cafés, and institutions—some of which are inspired by actual Savannah locations.

Real Savannah Locations That Inspired the Story

Falcon Square

Patricia's home faces a small fictional square named after her husband's family. It was inspired by the quieter, tucked-away squares like Troup Square and Pulaski Square, places where history lingers but tourists rarely go.

Gryoti's Office

Magnum Oncology's sleek, intimidating office was influenced by some of the high-end private practices along Abercorn Street—where polished stone lobbies and garden views mask the stress inside.

Patricia's Gala Venue

The gala in Chapter Five drew from the Harper Fowlkes House and Hotel Bardo—stately venues where Savannah's elite gather, and secrets hide behind champagne smiles.

Bonaventure Cemetery

Though not featured directly, the quiet eeriness of Bonaventure Cemetery shaped the emotional tone of Patricia's internal fears—especially her growing anxiety over mortality and loss.

The Medical Mystery Angle

Doctor Gryoti's medical scam—administering unapproved, ineffective drugs to desperate patients—was inspired by real cases of medical fraud, some shockingly close to home. I researched stories involving:

-Falsified credentials
-Fake cancer treatments
-Offshore banking and crypto laundering

The character of Gryoti is fictional, but the techniques he uses mirror real-world schemes uncovered by journalists, whistleblowers, and the FDA.

Creating Patricia Falcon

Patricia is a Southern woman of poise, intelligence, and fierce moral clarity. Her character was born from a blend of Savannah's gracious social culture and the tenacity of true crime investigators. She's a former beauty queen with grit, not gloss—and she's unafraid to ask hard questions, even in high society circles.

Her fear of losing her husband Trey evolved organically as the story progressed, shaped by real conversations I've had with readers and friends about how deeply personal justice— and grief—can be.

What's Real, What's Fiction?

-The drugs in the book—Blanscan, Stemase, and Dustare —are fictional, but they mirror actual fake drugs listed by the FDA.

-The Georgia Composite Medical Board subplot was inspired by real-world cases of officials being investigated for ethics violations.

-The emotional thread of facing a loved one's cancer, and the fear of being left behind, is deeply personal—and very real.

Naomi's Music

Naomi Gryoti, the gifted pianist, was inspired by several real finalists of the Hilton Head International Piano Competition—an event that truly celebrates emerging classical talent. Naomi's music is meant to show that even monsters like Gryoti can love, and that love can leave them vulnerable.

A Word from Alan Chaput

Writing Savannah Med pushed me into uncomfortable territory—researching medical fraud, legal technicalities, and facing the raw emotions of fear and injustice. But it also reminded me of the power of community, the strength of family, and the value of truth.

Savannah isn't just a backdrop. It's a living, breathing character in this story. And like Patricia, it holds history, hides secrets, and refuses to look away.

Thank you for reading.
—Alan

ACKNOWLEDGMENTS

First and foremost, I'm grateful to you for reading *Savannah Med* and hope you enjoyed it. You are the reason I write.

Thank you to Dr. Charles Lucas for giving me the idea for this story.

Thank you to Jason Lips for helping me with the choreography of the fight scene. Thank you to Lori Russell, RN for checking my oncology references. Thank you to Amy Coury for helping with the final edits.

Thank you to my editor, Elizabeth A. White, who not only improved my writing, grammar, and punctuation, but also fact-checked everything from law details to all things Savannah.

Thank you to the reviewers and bloggers who've so generously spread the word about *Savannah Med*, and who've taken the time to give readers an opinion about it.

And, most of all, thank you to Terri Chaput, my wife, for her patience, understanding, and support for my writing.

As you can see, it takes a team to produce a book, and I'm very grateful to be on this one.

ABOUT THE AUTHOR

Alan Chaput writes Southern mysteries. His novels have finaled in the Daphne and the Claymore. Al lives with his wife in Coastal South Carolina. When not writing, Al can be found Shag dancing, pursuing genealogy, or interacting on social media.

ALSO BY ALAN CHAPUT

Savannah Sleuth (Book 1)

Savannah Secrets (Book 2)

Savannah Justice (Book 3)

Savannah Dragon (Book 4)

Savannah Med (Book 5)

Savannah Christmas (Book 6 - coming 2026)